Hodder

a ed

For Megan Johnson with love and thanks

Published by Hodder Children's Books 2000

Edited by Nicola Barber
Consultant: Lloyd Readhead
Series designed by Fiona Webb
Book designed by Joy Mutter

10 9 8 7 6 5 4 3 2 1

A catalogue record for this book is available from the British Library.

ISBN: 0 340 77897 0

The information in this book has been thoroughly researched and checked for accuracy, and safety advice is given where appropriate. Neither the author nor the publishers can accept any responsibility for any loss, injury or damage incurred as a result of using this book.

Printed by Clays Ltd, St Ives plc.

Hodder Children's Books
a division of Hodder Headline Limited
338 Euston Road
London NW1 3BH

Meet the author

Caroline Plaisted is a freelance writer who has written over 20 books for children and adults on subjects varying from cookery and ballet to ponies and the weather. She first became fascinated by the sport of gymnastics as a child when she saw Olga Korbut take the world by storm at the Munich Olympics in 1972. When Caroline watched her niece, Megan, performing her gymnastic skills at a wedding reception she was inspired by this performance to write this book about the subject.

Introduction

Look at the gymnast move! Yes, that's it! A perfect 10! The gold medal is theirs!

It's impossible to watch international gymnasts competing without wanting to leap across the room and try to reach for the sky (and that gold medal) along with them. As the gymnasts roll, leap, flic-flac and turn, they appear to perform with effortless ease – as if they have hidden springs in their feet! But to get to this standard takes years of training, hard work, talent and dedication.

If you have always wanted to join this élite team of athletes, give gymnastics a twirl and get superfit and supple by reading this book. What are you waiting for? Get on that mat!

TOP TIP

If you come across a word or term you don't recognise, look it up in the glossary on pages 123-4.

Contents

1 The first gymnasts 6

2 Getting started 12

3 A bounce around the gym 19

4 Your first sessions 26

5 Roll over... and stand up! 43

6 Head over heels 53

7 Leap for the sky 59

8 Rhythmic gymnastics 74

9 New gym sports 83

10 Going for gold 92

11 Look out for . . . 103

Taking a tumble or reaching for the skies? 113

Want to know more? 116

Glossary 123

Index 125

1 The first gymnasts

Olympic Games • modern gymnastics • women gymnasts

Since the 1970s, gymnastics has been one of the most popular sports at the Olympic Games and other major international sporting events. The combination of grace and breathtaking athletic ability has left audiences in awe of young gymnasts' performances.

Gymnastics in the past

It has not just been in the last few decades that athletes have learned their gymnastic skills. Historians have found out that the first gymnasts performed in Ancient Egypt over 3000 years ago and that the Ancient Greeks and Romans were also keen on the sport. They know this from the evidence of ancient pots and paintings that depict gymnastic displays.

Springboard

Gymnastics first appeared nearly 3000 years ago at the Olympic Games in 766BC. The Games were held in Greece and the competitors performed naked!

Although the Ancient Greeks were keen on the Olympic Games, it was only boys and young men who actually took part in the activities. Girls could only watch in admiration. But as the Greek and Roman empires began to crumble, so did the popularity of gymnastics and the Olympic Games.

Springboard

The Greek word for 'naked' is gymnos *which is why the Ancient Greeks called their bare athletes 'gymnasts'. The words 'gymnastics' and 'gymnasium' come from the same word.*

For a long time, there were no organised gymnastics displays or competitions. In fact, by the end of the 17th century, the most likely place to find gymnastics being performed was in a theatre or market place. During this time, groups of wandering entertainers performed acrobatics, tumbling and juggling for the public. An old picture has been found which shows a group of acrobats jumping from a box across a real horse – presumably this is their version of the vaulting horse (see page 23)! Poor horse!

Modern gymnastics

It wasn't until the 19th century that the modern gymnastics movement began to take shape. Two men were independently responsible for this. In Germany, a soldier called Friedrich Ludwich Jahn started to teach his fellow officers body-building exercises using parallel bars and a high bar. In 1811, Jahn started an open-air gymnastics centre in Berlin. It soon became a popular meeting-place for gentlemen and officers to show off their athletic abilities.

Jahn's open-air gymnastics centre

At about the same time, in Sweden a man called Pehr Henrik Ling started to teach a style of gymnastics as a keep-fit activity that did not require any apparatus. Large groups of people met to perform open-air exercises. Ling's method became known as Swedish drill.

Springboard

Over 21,000 gymnasts from 39 countries turned up in Sweden in 1999 for the World Gymnaestrada. They ranged from toddlers to grannies and grandads, and they came from all over the world. Switzerland had the largest team of over 4000 gymnasts, Nigeria the smallest with only one. Look Gymnaestrada up on their website: ***www.gymnaestrada.com***

Jahn and Ling soon got to hear about each other's different teaching methods and they both strongly disapproved of the other's beliefs – so much so that they became enemies. Nowadays, gymnasts know that both men contributed to the various skills needed for modern gymnastics.

By the late 19th century, there was so much interest in gymnastics that in the first modern Olympic Games in Athens in 1896, the sport appeared as one of the nine selected disciplines. Women were still not allowed to take part as gymnastics wasn't considered to be a feminine activity. The men, meanwhile, competed in teams rather than as individual athletes.

Enter the women!

It wasn't until 1928 that women gymnasts competed in the Olympics. That year, they took part at the Amsterdam competition in team events. The Dutch women's team won the gold medal.

In 1952, the Olympic Games were held in Helsinki and women took part in individual overall championships for the first time. It was also the year that Russian gymnasts first appeared at the Games along with 300 other gymnasts from a total of 30 countries. By the late 1960s, Eastern European gymnasts dominated the sport and in the 1970s two gymnasts became the darlings of the sporting world, the Russian, Olga Korbut, and the Romanian, Nadia Comaneci.

Olga Korbut appeared at the 1972 Olympics and took the world by storm with her exciting musical and athletic style, and her elfin looks. Sadly, despite her undoubted skill which led her to win three gold medals, Olga Korbut failed to become the overall Olympic champion because of a disastrous fall on the asymmetric bars.

In 1978, Nadia Comaneci became the first gymnast to achieve the maximum score of ten out of ten. The whole world adored Nadia and she became known in the press as 'Little Miss Perfect'. She won five Olympic gold medals.

Both Olga Korbut and Nadia Comaneci caught the public imagination and gym clubs opened all around the world. It is thanks to people like Nadia and Olga, and more recently Shannon Miller, that you are now reading this book and planning your own Olympic career!

2 Getting started

Young gymnasts • what to wear • getting the kit • finding a club

What age can I get started?

Maybe you've seen some gymnasts dazzling the audience on the television, or maybe you've had your first session on the gym equipment at school. Either way, you want to get started!

These days you can begin some form of organised gymnastics almost as soon as you can walk and run. Most local sports and leisure centres have a gymnastics training programme and their youngest classes will probably be for toddlers and children of pre-school age. In the UK, British Gymnastics has a popular network of pre-school classes for the young gymnast. In Australia, Kindergym is the youngest branch of the Australian Gymnastics Federation. Other countries also run extensive gymnastics programmes. You can find out more about these organisations on pages 116-18.

What qualities and abilities will I need for gymnastics?

Well, you obviously need to be interested in the sport. But you also need to be generally fit and agile with supple limbs – although your training will help to improve all of these abilities. If you want to go on to take part at competition and display level, you will need to be prepared to train and practise hard, and have a lot of discipline and determination. Gymnasts need to have a natural ability to stand with their back straight so that they neither hunch their shoulders forward, nor stick their bottom out.

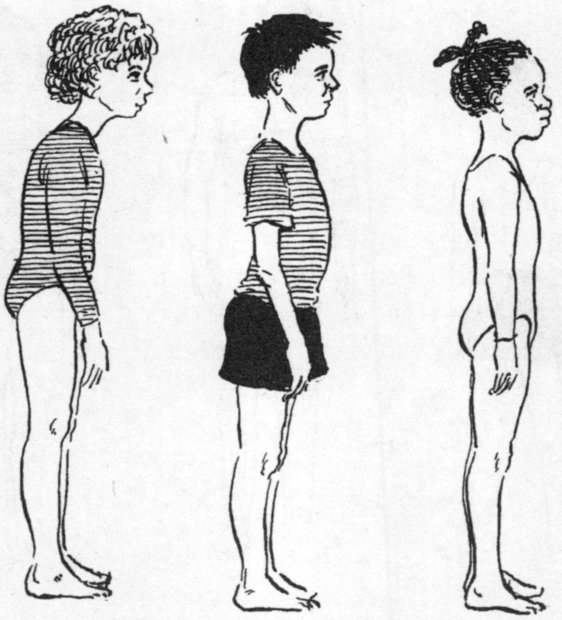

✗ ✗ ✓

Gymnasts also need to be able to move rhythmically and naturally, and look like they are enjoying themselves despite all the effort and hard work they are putting into their sport!

What do I need to wear for my first session?

You will need to be comfortable and warm without being too hot for your first session. Both boys and girls can start in gymnastics by wearing shorts and a T-shirt. As they progress, girls train in long-sleeved leotards made of close-fitting stretchy fabric. These allow your coach (and later your audience) to see your body moving properly and allow you to have freedom of movement.

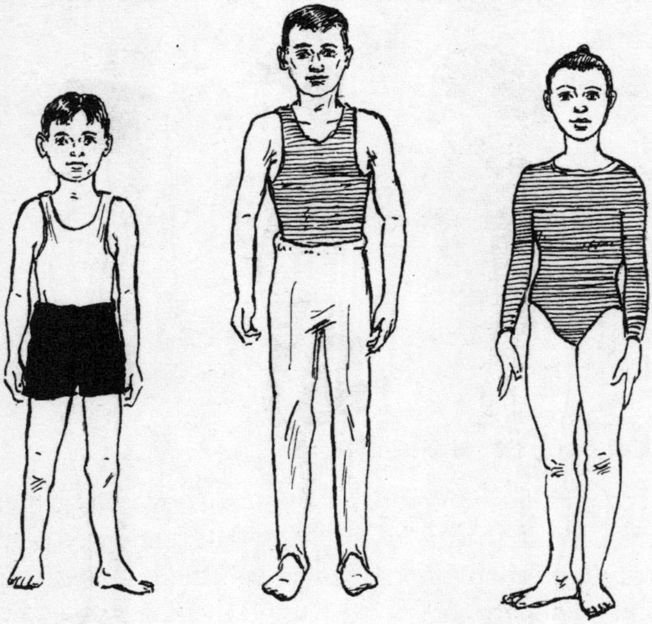

Boys usually wear a tight-fitting sleeveless leotard or vest and a pair of shorts. Once they enter competitions, the boys continue to wear this outfit for floorwork and vaulting, but must wear long trousers rather than shorts for the other apparatus.

You will also need to have a tracksuit to wear over your practice clothes. This will keep you warm while you wait for your training session to begin. Your coach may ask you to wear your tracksuit while you do your warm-up exercises at the beginning of the session.

Springboard

The first leotard was worn in the 19th century by Jules Léotard who invented the outfit. Jules was a French acrobatic trapeze artist who was fed up with wearing two-piece outfits which came apart in the middle as he was flying through the air! Sadly for Jules, it was his outfit rather than his ability as a gymnast that made him famous.

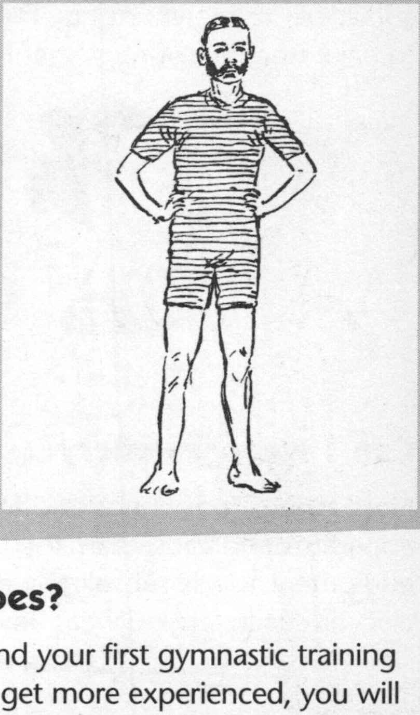

Do I need to wear shoes?

Your coach will ask you to attend your first gymnastic training sessions without shoes. As you get more experienced, you will progress to wearing gymnastic slippers but your coach will tell you when you are ready to start using them. However, right from the start you will need a pair of training shoes to wear to and from your training sessions and any time that you are waiting around in the gym. Make sure that your trainers have non-marking soles so that they don't damage the gymnasium floor.

What do I do with my hair?

Make sure that your hair is neat and tidy. Both boys and girls with long hair should tie it back in a pony tail or plait so that it doesn't fall into their eyes. If your hair is very long, you may want to secure a plait so that it doesn't hit you (or your coach!) in the eyes as you twist and turn across the gym.

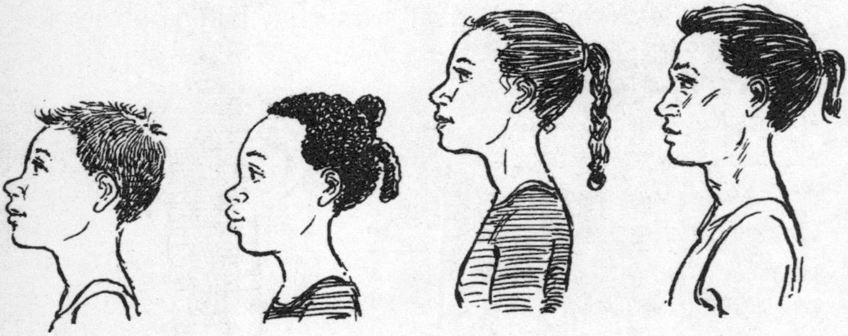

Can I wear jewellery?

No! Earrings, nose rings and finger rings can catch on the apparatus and cause damage to both your body and the equipment. Under absolutely no circumstances will your club or coach let you wear any jewellery.

Off the mat

Your gym club or national or local training squad may well have their own club colours or design for leotards and tracksuits. Ask your coach for advice about this. He or she will also be able to advise you about the best places to buy your clothes and equipment.

Do I need any other kit?

At first, all you need is a bag to keep your practice clothes in, and a towel to wipe yourself down with when you are hot. In time, if you start working on the bars and the rings, your coach will advise you to buy handguards. These are necessary to help you grip the bars and to help with swinging and circling movements. They will also prevent you getting blisters from the movement of your hands on the apparatus. The handguards that boys wear are slightly different from the ones that girls wear.

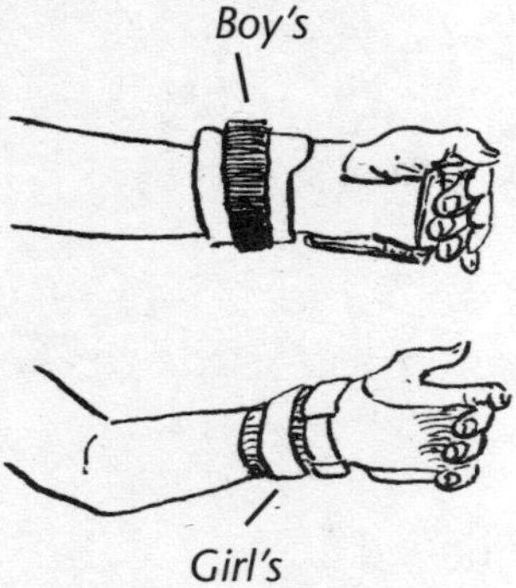

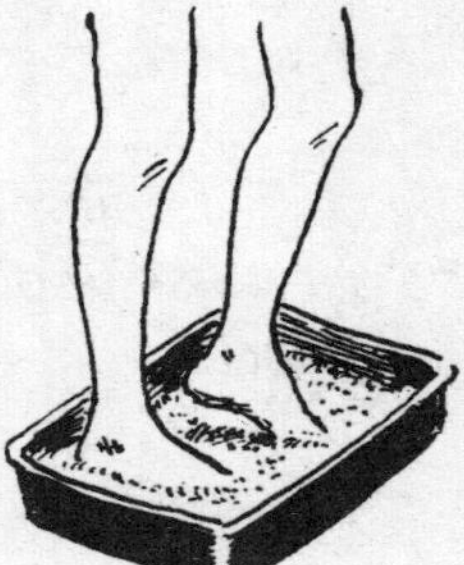

The gym will provide chalk for you to rub into the soles of your feet and palms of your hands. This will stop you from getting sticky with sweat and slipping on the floor and apparatus.

How do I find the right club?

There will probably be a club at your local leisure or sports centre and the first thing you should do is arrange to go along to watch a training session before you join up. Ask if the coaches are qualified, and if they are members of the gymnastic governing body for your country (you can find out more about these organisations on pages 116-18).

These are the signs of a good gym club:

- *The gymnasium should be clean with the apparatus laid out in an organised fashion.*
- *The apparatus should be in good condition.*
- *The gymnasts should be properly dressed with a neat and tidy appearance. Their hair should be tied back and they shouldn't be wearing any jewellery.*
- *The gymnasium should be properly lit.*
- *The club should have a code of practice or rules of the gym. Ask about this when you speak to the club coach.*
- *The coaches should be qualified.*
- *The coaches should be willing to tell you about the awards and competitions entered by club members. You may not want to take part in these, but they should be available to you in case you want to test your ability as you progress.*
- *The gymnasts should be having fun!*

3 A bounce around the gym

The three branches • the apparatus

You will feel a lot more confident about your first session if you know what the main pieces of apparatus are and what they are used for. Gymnastics is divided into three main branches:

- Artistic (which uses fixed apparatus)
- Rhythmic (which uses hand-held apparatus)
- Sports acrobatics and tumbling (which uses a sprung strip of floor and sometimes a springboard)

Boys and girls take part in separate exercises and competitions. You can find out more about each of the three main gymnastic disciplines in the relevant chapters later in the book.

Rhythmic

Artistic

Sports acrobatics

Off the mat

Never forget that it is dangerous to use any of the apparatus until you have enough experience and supervision. Your coach will tell you when you are ready and will help you to use the apparatus safely. Remember, your coach knows best!

What sort of apparatus will I find in the gym?

Some apparatus is used by both girls and boys and some is unique to the boys or used slightly differently by the girls. This picture shows you how a competition arena is laid out ready for use by all the gymnasts.

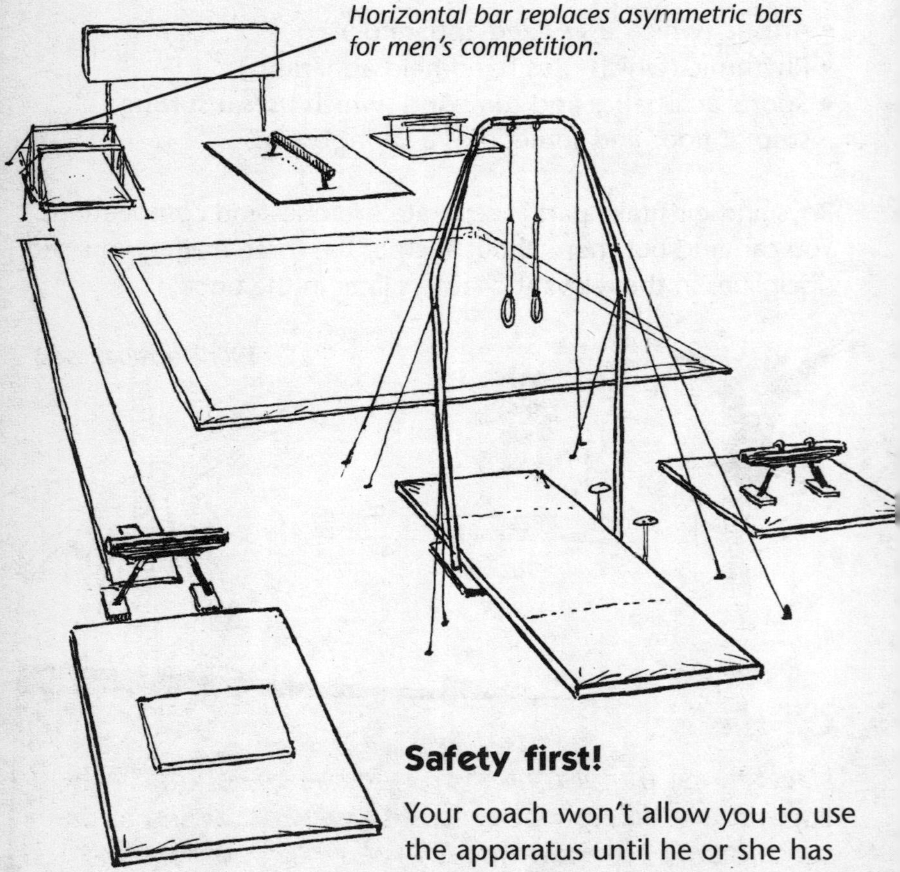

Safety first!

Your coach won't allow you to use the apparatus until he or she has checked that the safety wires and chains (not shown here) are secure.

The floor

Floor exercises take place on an area 12 metres square which has a special carpeted surface. The floor area has a springy base and is bordered by a white line. Unlike boys, girls perform their floor routines to music.

Asymmetric bars

The asymmetric bars are used only by girls, who work in swings and handstands around and over both of the bars.

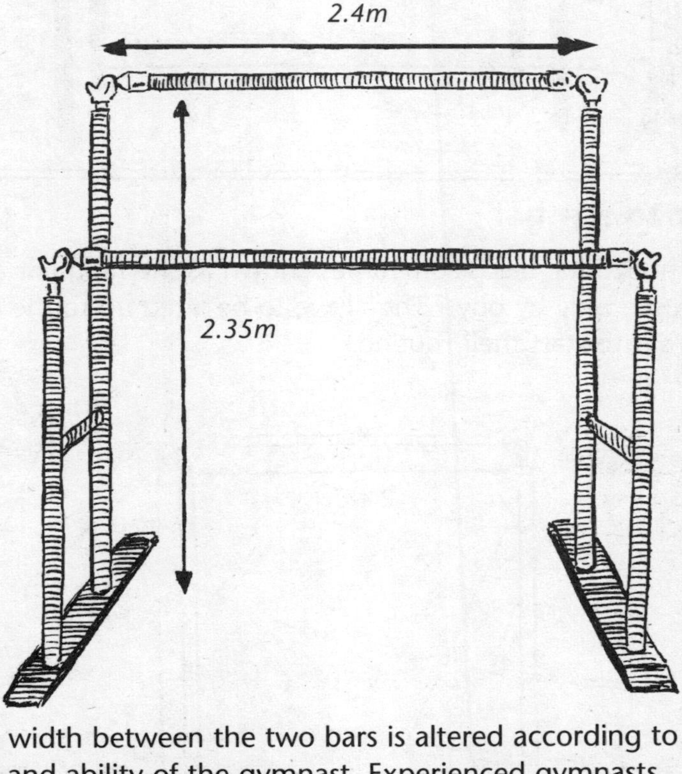

The width between the two bars is altered according to the age and ability of the gymnast. Experienced gymnasts perform moves in which they let go of the bar, carry out a move in the air, and then catch hold of the bar again!

Parallel bars

The parallel bars are for boys only. They swing between and above them.

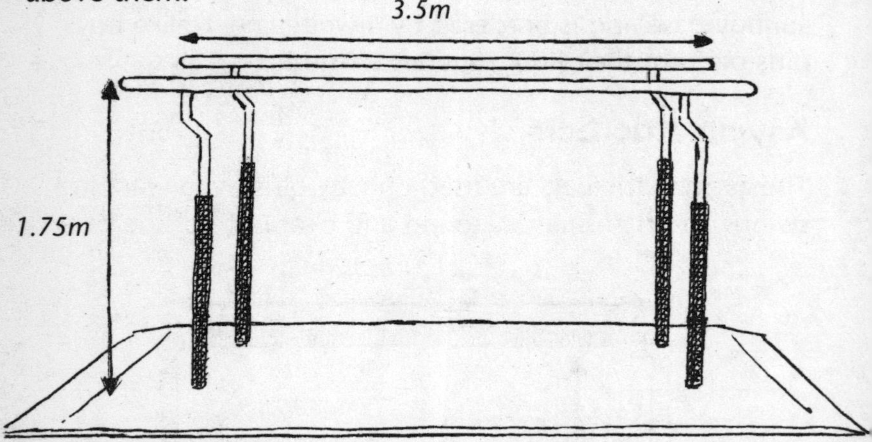

Horizontal bar

The horizontal bar is sometimes known as the high bar and it is used only by boys. They have to be lifted up to the bar in order to start their routine.

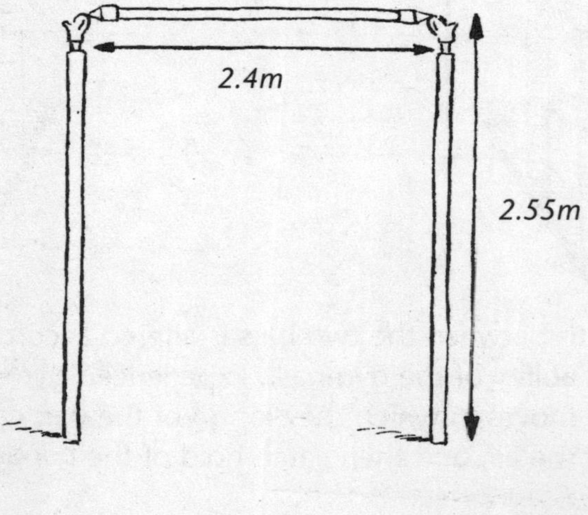

The horse

The horse is used by both boys and girls but in different ways. Girls use the horse as a broad horse and vault across its suede, non-slip surface. Boys use the horse as a long horse so that they vault along it. The horse is 10 centimetres higher for boys.

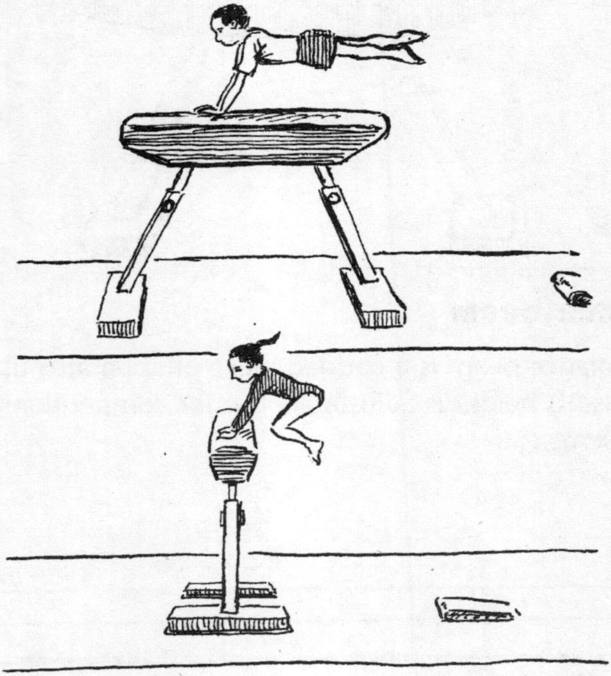

Springboard

Until the 1930s, the vaulting horse was shaped exactly like a real horse!

Pommel horse

The pommel horse stands 115cm high. It is used only by boys. They swing their bodies across the horse supported by their hands on the handles.

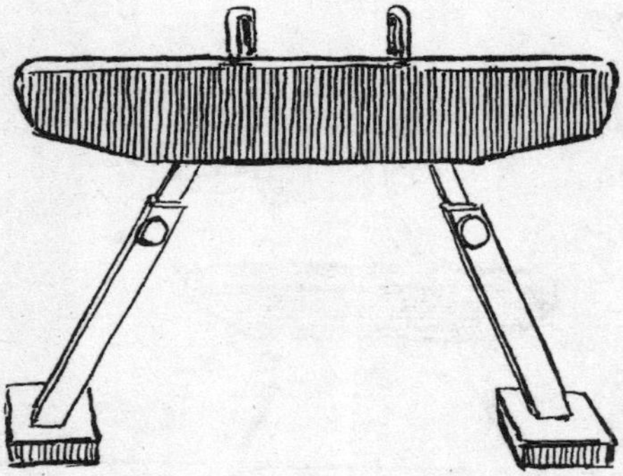

Balance beam

The balance beam is a padded piece of apparatus used only by girls. Its height is adjustable, but for competitions it is set at 120cm.

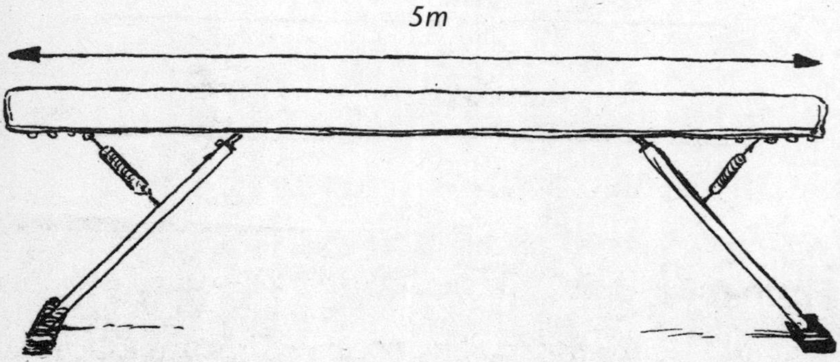

The rings

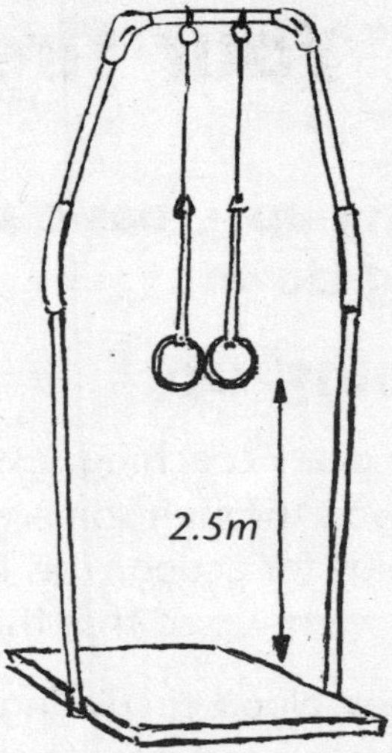

Until the 1950s, the rings were used by girls as well as boys, but they are now an exclusively male zone. The rings are for the men to display swinging movements with strength and control. The rings themselves are not meant to swing.

Springboard

Gymnasts use the springboard to rebound upwards and forwards when vaulting or when using the beam and asymmetric bars.

Will I be able to use all this equipment straight away?

No. Your coach will gradually help you to build up your skill and strength so that you can progress to using different bits of apparatus. You will also need to develop your flexibility and suppleness before you can start to copy the fantastic displays of the gymnasts you watch on the television and at competitions.

4 Your first sessions

Warming up • basic shapes • balancing • cooling down

Warming up

Before every coaching session in the gym, your coach will take you through some warm-up exercises to get your body ready for action. This is very important. All athletes need to warm-up so that they can:

- Get their blood circulating more quickly through their body.
- Make their heart beat faster ready for exercise.
- Loosen up their muscles.
- Loosen up their joints.

Off the mat

Remember that it is dangerous to do any form of gymnastics without warming up. If you don't warm up properly, you risk pulling muscles and tendons and causing long-term or even permanent injury!

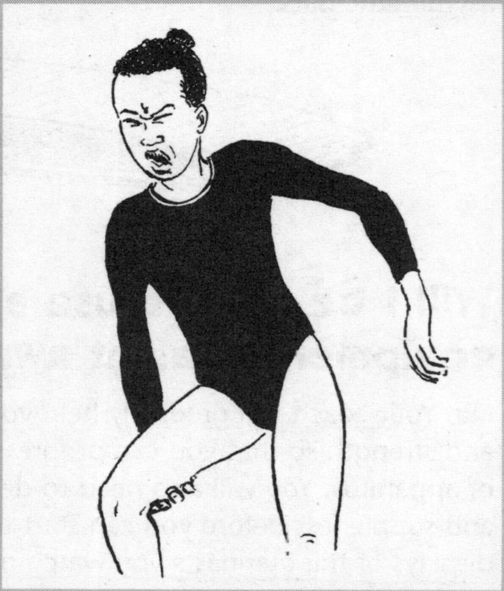

Your coach will have his or her own warm-up routine which he or she will explain to you at your first session. Listen carefully to what your coach says and do exactly what they ask.

If you practise your warm-up exercises at home, remember to always do them correctly. Never be tempted to skip an exercise because you don't think it's necessary – your coach has the experience to know what routine you should follow.

It's just as important to look after your body after exercising as it is before. See page 42 for more about what you should do at the end of a session in the gym.

Off the mat

Don't worry if some of your muscles feel slightly sore after a gym session. This is because you've been using your body to do new things. A warm bath will help to ease the soreness. However, if you've got a persistent pain or ache, discuss it with your coach who will advise you whether you should see a doctor or a physiotherapist.

Off the mat

Before you start your warm-up routine, raise your body temperature by gently moving your body. First, lightly shake your arms and legs. Then swing your shoulders a few times together, and separately. Next, flex the fingers on both hands by spreading them and contracting them back into a ball. Finally, flex your feet by moving them as if you are jogging on the spot – but without lifting your feet from the floor. Now you should be ready to start your warm-up.

What exercises can I do to warm up?

Here are some simple warm-up exercises:

STEP 1 ▶

First of all sit on the floor with your legs straight out in front of you like this:

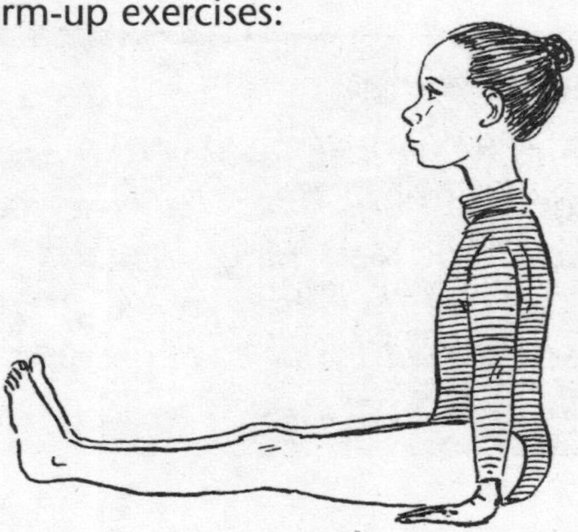

STEP 2 ▶

Now point your toes down towards the floor like this:

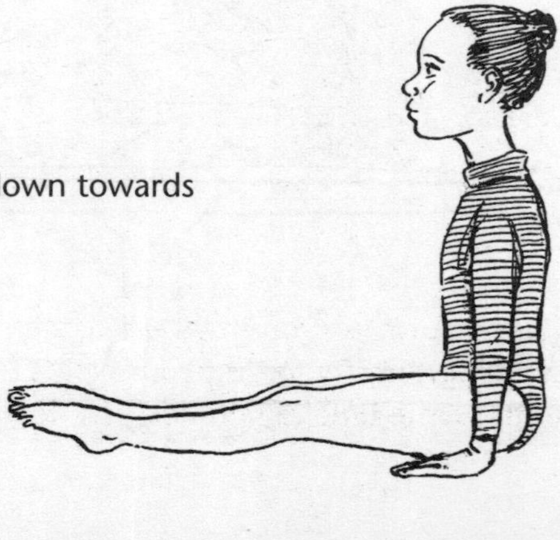

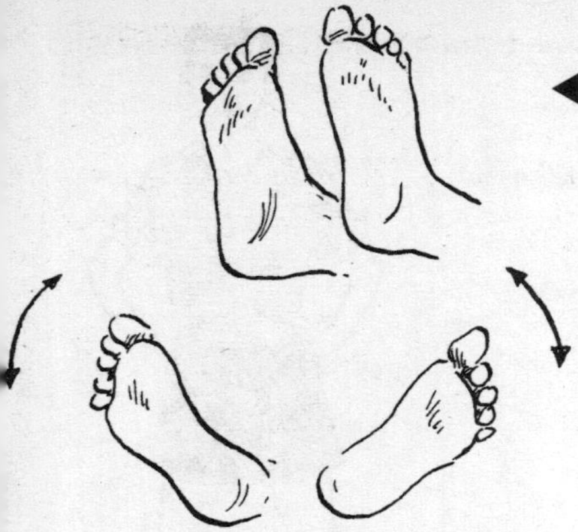

STEP 3

Flex your toes up and down about ten times. Variations on this exercise would be to flex your feet upwards but with only the toes turned up, or to rotate your feet from the ankle in a circular movement.

STEP 1

You can also warm up and flex your feet by standing with your legs together and your feet facing the front. Make sure your arms are outstretched like this:

STEP 2

Now rise up on to your toes like this:

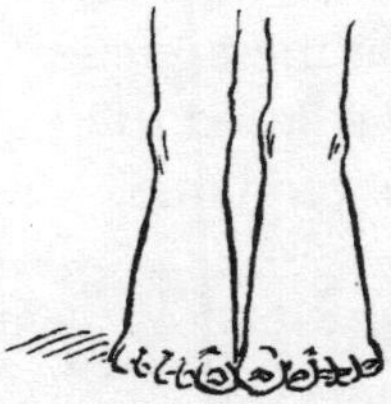

Flex up and down on your toes at least ten times. When you get used to doing this, try flexing your hands up and down at the wrist at the same time as you flex your feet!

STEP 1 ▶

Now flex your waist. Stand with your feet apart and your hands on your hips like this:

STEP 2 ▶

Then lean over towards your right like this:

Return to the upright position before you bend over towards your left. Repeat the exercise so that you have flexed to each side about ten times.

Off the mat

Don't panic if you can't do each warm up ten times. Do as many as you can to start with, and then build up the numbers as you become more flexible and have more stamina.

Other variations on this exercise include holding one hand on your waist or thigh and then flexing over towards that hand while holding the other arm up and above your head like this:

You can also hold your hands on your hips and flex your body by leaning forwards and then upright again.

What happens after I've warmed up?

Your coach will take you at your pace through some basic skills and shapes. It is very important for you to perfect your floor skills before you start trying to work on the apparatus. The shapes that you learn first will form the basis of the rest of your gymnastic career. Whatever shapes or skills you perform, always:

- Keep feet that are off the floor pointed.
- Keep your hands fully flexed along the length of your fingers.
- Try not to show any tension and strain in your face.

What are the basic shapes I need to learn?

Let's tackle the simplest shapes first:

Front scale

Stand on one leg and stretch your arms out at the side. Now lift one leg up in front of you, remembering to keep both your arms and legs straight. You need to perfect this shape using either leg in front.

Back scale

This is the opposite of front scale. Try to keep your balance straight up through the centre of your body and out of the top of your head so that you don't lean too far over to one side.

Off the mat

In all the basic shapes where you need to keep your body upright, try to imagine that you are a puppet with an invisible piece of string attached to your head. The puppeteer is pulling your string up towards the ceiling, helping you to keep your balance centred and your back lengthened.

Dish

Lie on your back on the mat with your arms resting along your body and your hands resting on your thighs. Now tuck your chin into your chest and curl your head off the floor. At the same time lift up your legs, making sure that your feet are together and pointed.

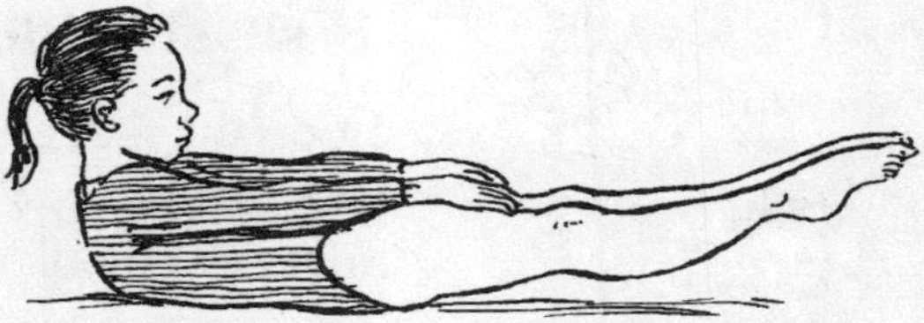

This shape can also be performed with your arms held above your head and with your face pointing up to the ceiling.

Arch

This is the opposite position to the dish because this time you are lying on your front on the mat and curving your back. Just like the dish, you need to keep your feet together but this time you also want to make sure that your arms are fully stretched and your eyes are looking ahead of you and not down to the floor.

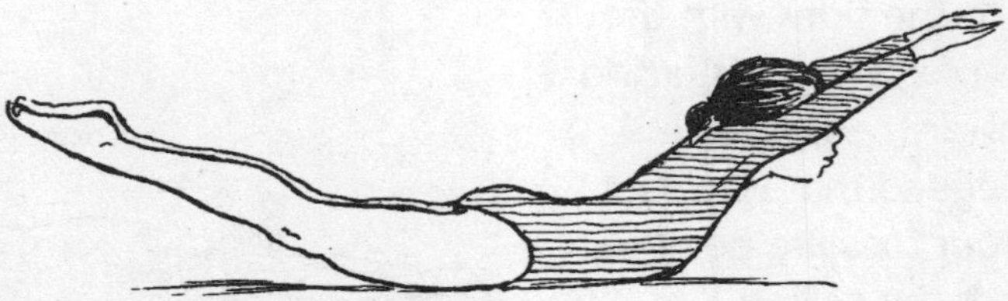

'L' sit piked

Sit on the mat with your legs stretched out in front of you and raise your arms above your head. Try to make sure that your knees are 'pressing' into the floor.

'L' sit straddled

Sit on the mat and stretch your feet out towards your sides. You should have your arms raised above your head.

Try to make sure that your knees point towards the ceiling and don't roll in towards the floor. You will find that the more you practise this shape, the easier it will be to extend your legs out in line with your hips. This shape is sometimes called the box splits and you may be asked to hold your arms out towards your sides instead of above your head.

'L' lie

Lie on your back on the mat and position your arms to the sides with the palms of your hands facing downwards. Now raise your legs so that your feet and your toes are pointing towards the ceiling.

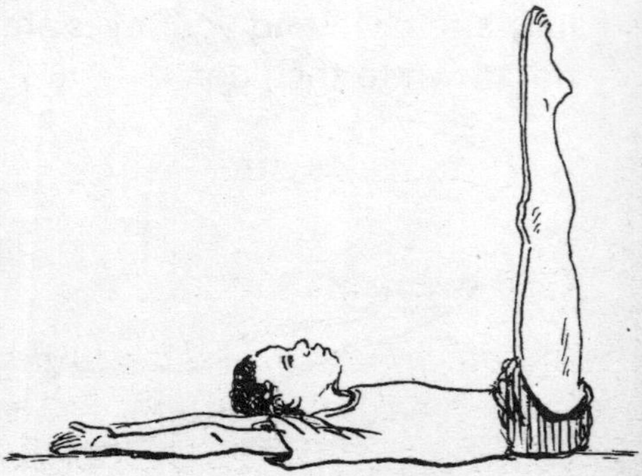

Front support

Facing the mat, you will need to put your hands a shoulders-width apart with the palms down on the mat. Position your legs straight out behind you and suspend the weight of your body on your arms – but make sure that you keep your arms straight.

Back support

This is the opposite of the front support. This time, with your palms facing down on the mat, push your hips up towards the ceiling. Make sure that you don't arch your back and that your fingers point towards your feet.

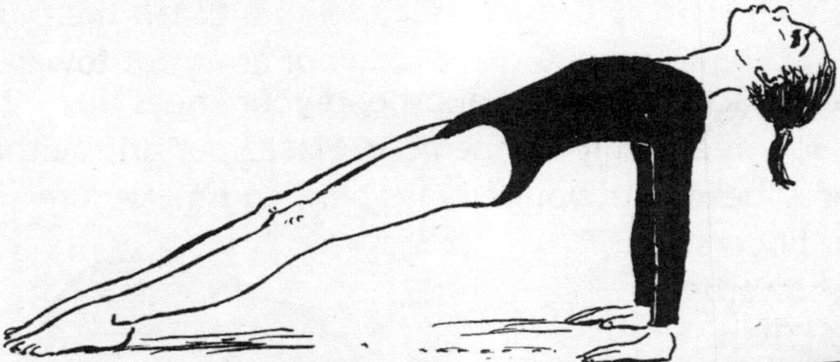

Off the mat

In both the front and back supports, make sure that your body is held in a straight line and that you don't curve your back either upwards or downwards in the middle.

What are the more difficult shapes I need to learn?

Once you've got to grips with the shapes you've just read about, your coach may let you try working on these:

Shoulder stand

Lie on your back on the floor with your hands above your head. Make sure the backs of your hands are on the floor and your palms are pointing up towards the ceiling. With your toes pointed and your legs outstretched, raise your legs up and continue moving them up towards the ceiling so that your hips come up next and finally you are resting your weight on your shoulders.

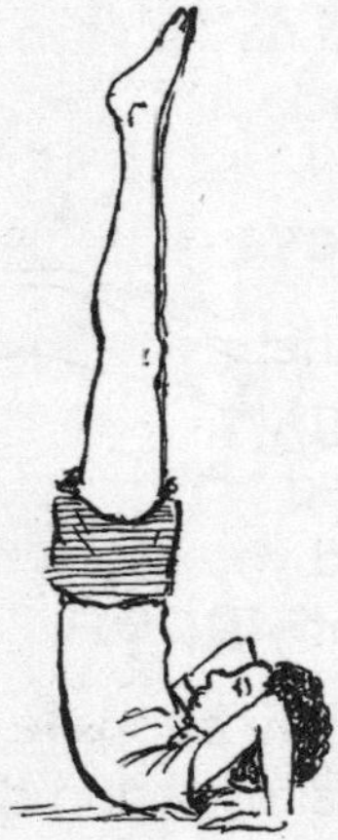

Bridge

Lie on your back on the mat and bend your knees up keeping your feet firmly on the floor. Place your arms either side of your head with your elbows bent and make sure that your fingers are pointing towards your feet. Then push your body up towards the ceiling so that you are taking your body's weight on your feet and hands.

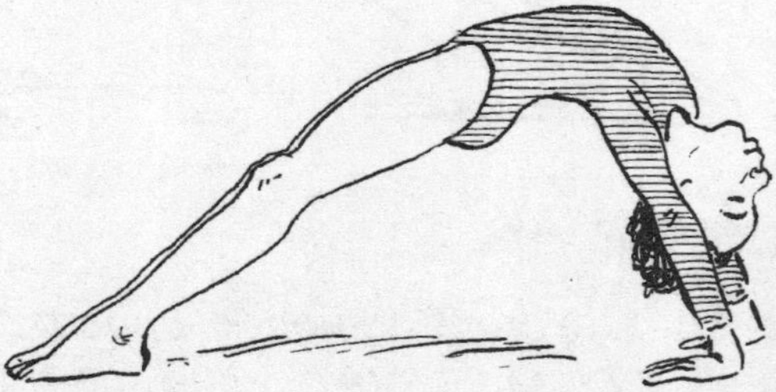

Kneeling on one leg

Position yourself so that you are kneeling on all fours. Looking ahead of you, raise one leg behind you, remembering to point your feet and not to over-arch your back.

Half lever

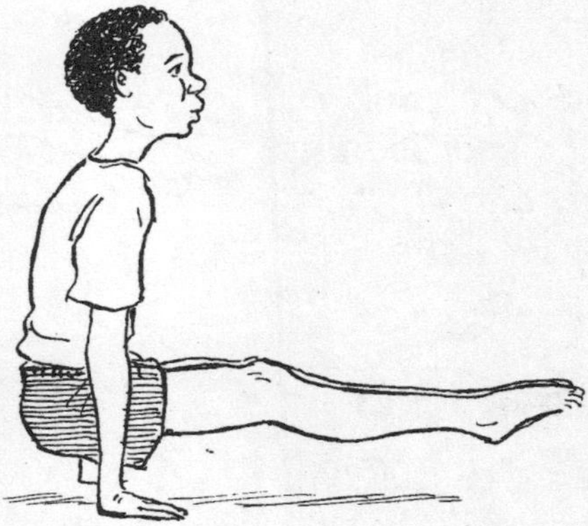

Sit on the mat with your legs out-stretched in front of you and your arms down at your sides. Make sure your hands are palms down on the mat with your fingers pointing down to your toes. Now, lift your body weight on to the palms of your hands.

Off the mat

All gymnasts continue to practise these basic shapes throughout their careers. The more you work on your gymnastics, the more supple you will become and the easier you will find it to perform difficult manouevres. You also need to perfect the basic shapes before you can begin to try them out on the apparatus.

Advanced moves

These are difficult moves, so you mustn't try them until your coach thinks you are ready. Instead, watch the older gymnasts at your club. Read about the technicalities here, and then decide what marks you would give them out of ten!

Straddle hold

The gymnast sits on the mat in the 'L' sit straddle position (see page 34). She puts her hands palm down on the floor in front of her and lifts her body weight on to her palms.

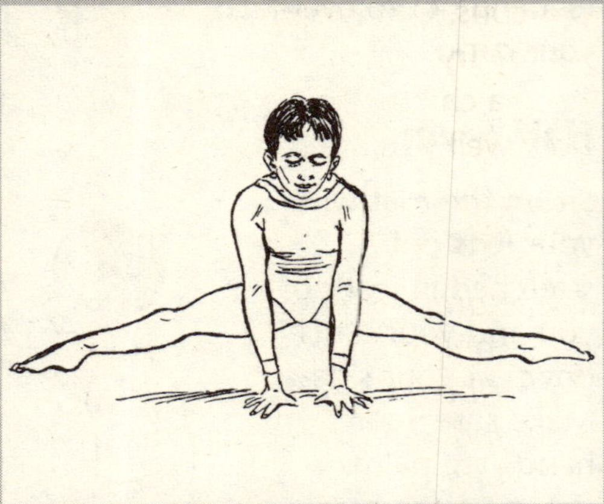

Russian lever

This is a difficult one. The gymnast must keep his shoulders down but without tucking his chin into his chest, or tilting his head back.

I'm very wobbly! What can I do to stop this?

Learn to balance! Again, it's practice that makes perfect, and there is no substitute for it. When you first learn the basic shapes, time yourself to see how long you can hold the positions. Can you hold them for five seconds? Ten seconds? More? Try to hold them for longer each time you do them. Keep a chart at home so that when you practise you know how well you are progressing.

Off the mat

These are the principles of balancing:

- *Be composed – have a clear head and think only of your balancing.*
- *Extend your stretch right out to the tips of your fingers and toes.*
- *Keep control of your muscles – pull in your stomach and bottom muscles.*
- *Breathe! An intake of breath will help you to compose a shape with your body. But if you don't breathe out and then breathe in again you'll not only go purple in the face – you could pass out! Breathing properly means that the oxygen will get to your head and through to your muscles allowing your body to work fully and effectively.*

What other balances are there?

You've already learned how to balance on one knee and two hands (see page 37). Once you have perfected this, you can move on to balancing on one foot and no hands.

STEP 1 ▶

First of all, try keeping your hands out at your sides and then drawing one leg up in front of you like this:

◀ **STEP 2**

If your arms are in the correct position they will help you to balance. Once you are able to hold this position comfortably and without wobbling, try turning your raised leg out to the side like this:

STEP 3 ▶

Remember the imaginary piece of string that is pulling you up through your head! When you are able to hold this position, try extending your raised leg out to your side like this:

Off the mat

Many gymnasts find that ballet lessons help them to improve their gymnastic skills. Some ballet steps mirror those performed by gymnasts, and the barre and floor-work in ballet help with balance and poise. Gymnasts have also found that doing a regular ballet class helps them to improve their flexibility and strength.

'V' sit balance

STEP 1 ▶

You'll need a lot of strength in your abdomen and thighs for this one. Start by sitting upright but with your hands resting on the floor.

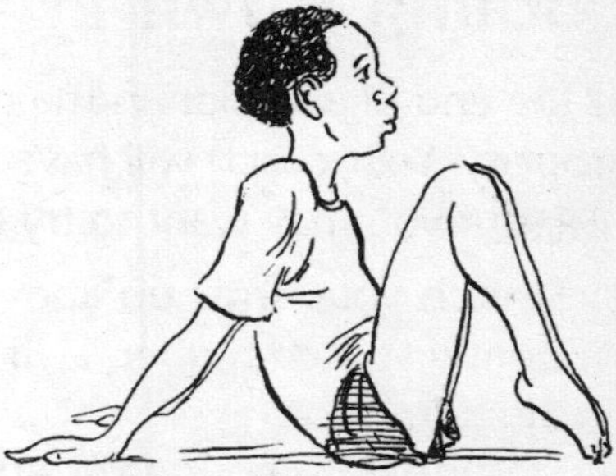

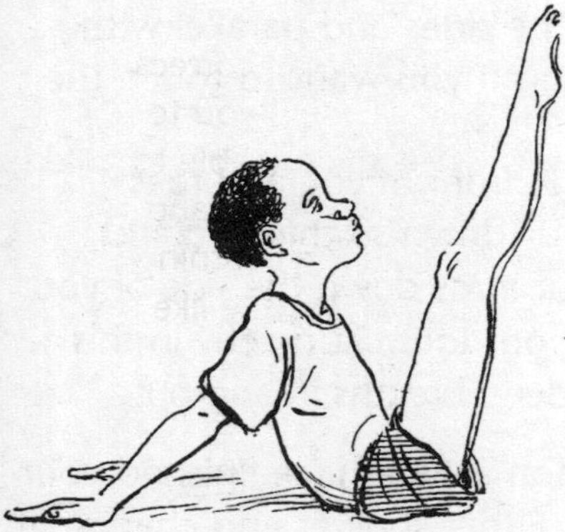

◀ **STEP 2**

Now, leaving your hands on the floor behind you, raise your legs up in front of you like this:

STEP 3 ▶

If you stretch your legs upwards and right through to your toes, and keep your eyes looking up to your toes, you will find it easier to balance. Once you are happy with the balance, take your arms up and out at your sides like this:

Remember to keep looking up and to have your abdominal muscles clenched as this will help you to lift your body up to create the V-shape. Oh, and make sure that you don't arch your back either!

Cooling down

At the end of a session in the gym, you should always cool down properly. Your coach will have a routine that he or she will teach you, but you may want to try these wind-down exercises:

- Stretch your arms up above your head as far as you can. Gently stretch higher, as if you are trying to reach through the gym roof.
- Starting with your arms above your head, move them down so that they are out at the sides and parallel with your shoulders. Stretch them, as if you want to touch the walls of the gym.
- Sit on the floor with your legs in front of you and toes pointed. Gently lower your body down so that you are folded over your legs, with your arms down the side of your legs and your hands hugging your toes. Sit quietly in this position while you take a few deep breaths in and out.

Remember to dress warmly as soon as you have finished your training session and wind-down. Either shower and change at the gym, or put on your tracksuit and trainers straight away, and have a warm bath or shower when you get home.

Off the mat

You'll get ahead more quickly in gymnastics if you remember these important things:

- *Always warm up and cool down properly.*
- *Never ignore your coach's instructions.*
- *Follow the rules of your gym club.*
- *Watch the more experienced members of your club and follow their example.*
- *Learn the basic shapes.*
- *Practise as often as possible.*

5 Roll over . . . and stand up!

Rolling • headstands & handstands

Now that you've got to grips with the basic gymnastic shapes, you can start to link them together. One of the first ways to do this is with rolls. When rolling, you are transferring your weight from one part of your body to another.

Which roll shall I try first?

Try a **half roll** like this one.

STEP 1 ▶
Start by squatting down on the mat. Balance on your toes and keep your arms out in front of you in line with your shoulders.

◀ **STEP 2**
Start to roll backwards by dropping your weight down on to your heels. Your bottom should touch the mat next and, as soon as it does, bend your arms behind you so that your hands can start to take your weight as you begin to roll.

STEP 3 ▶
You should roll back on to your shoulders and hands and have your hips in the air with your chest tucked into your chin. But this is as far as you go into the roll! You should let your weight roll you forwards again, back into your starting position, like this:

How do I complete the roll?

STEP 1 ▶

When you are completely in control of the half roll you can complete the first two steps of it and then continue to move backwards by letting your legs carry on over your head into a **backward roll**. Push up from the mat as strongly as you can and then, as your legs pass over your head, make sure that you tuck them in behind your head.

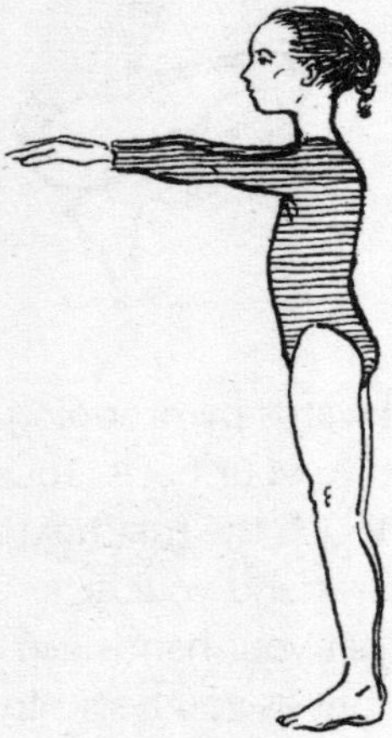

◀

STEP 2

You mustn't let your knees touch the floor. You should land the roll in the squatting position that you started in. Then straighten your legs and stand up.

Off the mat

If you think backwards you will move in a backwards direction! In the same way, thinking forwards will help you to get your body into the momentum of moving forwards!

Springboard

Your coach may let you use a wedge-shape of foam to practise your rolling on. This looks a bit like a large piece of cheese and its slope is useful when you are first learning to roll your weight backwards. By using a slope to do a backward roll you will find it easier to lean your weight backwards. This will let you concentrate on keeping your body in the right position and, once you have perfected this, you can then go on to learn to transfer your body weight.

How do I go forwards?

STEP 1 ▶

For a **forward roll**, start in the squat position with your arms in front of you.

STEP 2 ▶

Now, lean forwards and put your weight on the palms of your hands. As you lean forwards, keep your knees bent and tuck your head in towards your knees like this:

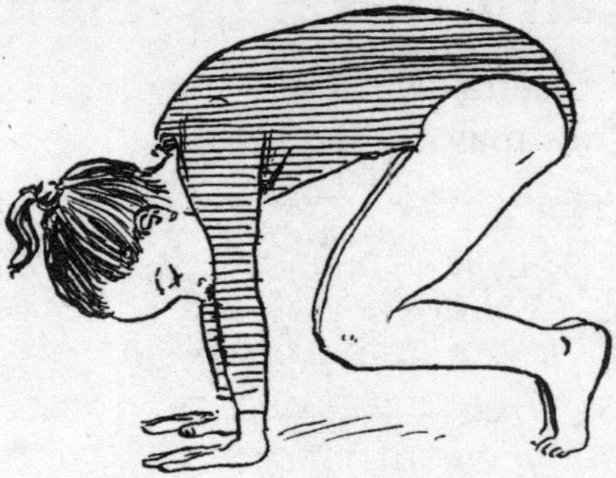

STEP 3 ▶

As you start to roll, push your weight up from the balls of your feet and continue to roll your weight forwards. Remember to keep your knees neatly tucked in like this:

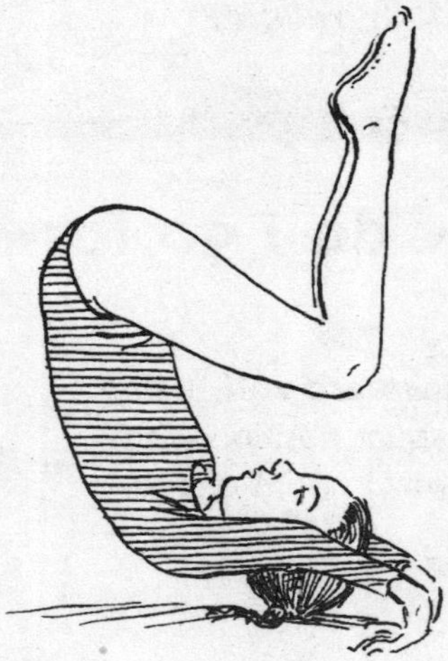

Finally come back into the squatting position and stand up with your arms out in front of you.

Can I travel in any other direction?

You certainly can. First try the **log roll** – and this isn't a Christmas pudding treat!

STEP 1

Begin by lying on the mat in an arch (see page 33).

▶

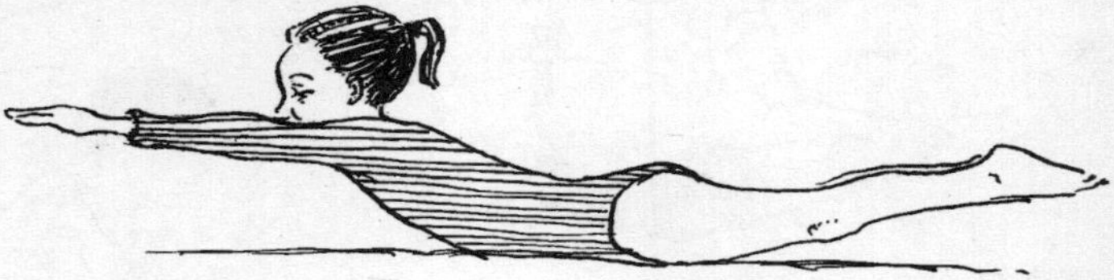

STEP 2

Keeping your body fully stretched, roll on to your side and then on to your back.

▶

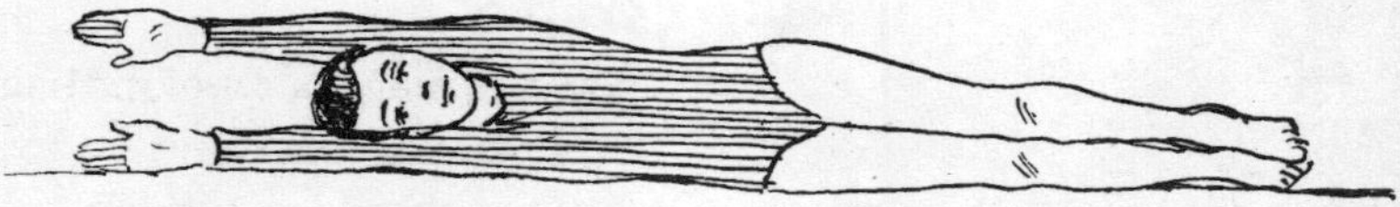

STEP 3

In the finishing position, you should make sure that the small of your back is pressed into the mat and isn't arched up.

▶

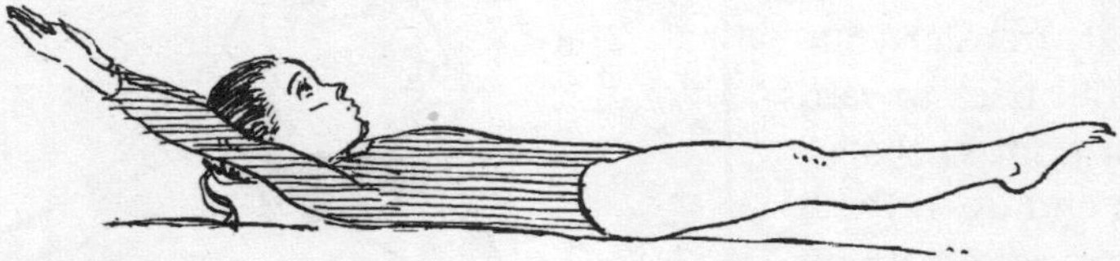

You can also perform a log roll by starting on your back and rolling on to your stomach. You can obviously roll either to your left or right.

A **circle roll** ends in the same position that it starts in, only you will be facing a different direction.

STEP 1

Start in an 'L' sit straddle with your hands resting on your knees.

STEP 2

Roll over down your right arm so that your weight is resting on to your right shoulder and your bottom is beginning to lift up.

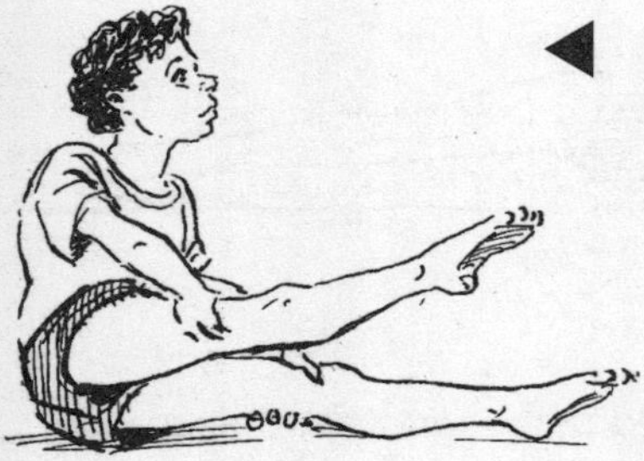

STEP 3

Now transfer your weight back through your back and on to your left shoulder, turning round as you do. Use the weight of your legs in the air to help you roll.

STEP 4

Finally transfer your weight back towards your right so that you end up in the 'L' sit straddle that you started in, only facing the other direction.

How do I stand on my head and hands?

Your coach will help you to get into your first **handstand** because you need strength in your arms and good balance.

STEP 1 ▶

Start by standing with one foot pointed in front of you and your arms stretched up through to your fingers above your head, like this:

◀ **STEP 2**

Lean forwards on to your pointed foot so that it is flat on the mat, and bend your knee. Keep your arms in the same position with your head still between them. Look towards the floor but slightly ahead of you – you are aiming to land your hands on the spot that you are looking at.

STEP 3 ▶

Keeping your hands shoulder-width apart on the mat, take your body weight on to your hands but keeping your arms straight. Push up from the foot that is on the floor and use the weight of that leg and the leg that is in the air to draw them up so that they are above your head. Your coach will help to support you as both legs come together above you.

Keep looking down at your hands and remember to point your toes so that you continue the same line throughout your body.

Off the mat

When you first learn a new move, your coach will always be there with you to support you with their hands. This is known as spotting and it will help you to feel safe and learn the full progression of a movement from start to finish. Once your coach is confident that you have learned a particular skill, they will let you complete it without spotting.

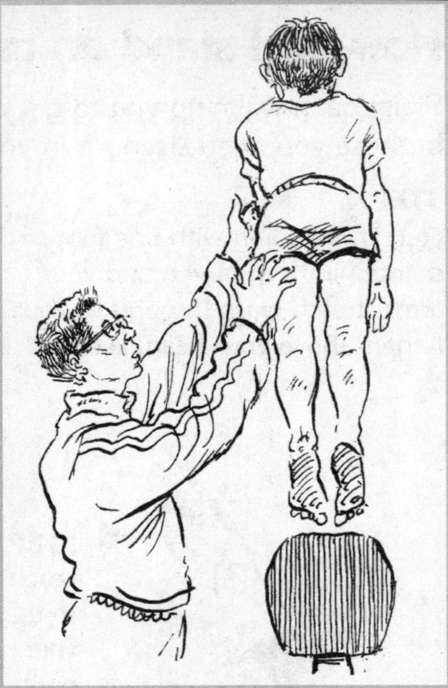

You can try doing a **headstand** against a wall.

STEP 1 ▶

Facing the wall, crouch down on the mat and then position your hands on the mat, tucking in your head between your hands. Push up from your feet to bring your hips in line above your head. Keep your knees tucked in towards your head and try to hold the balance.

STEP 2 ▶

When you are ready, try lifting your legs up so that your body forms a line parallel to the wall.

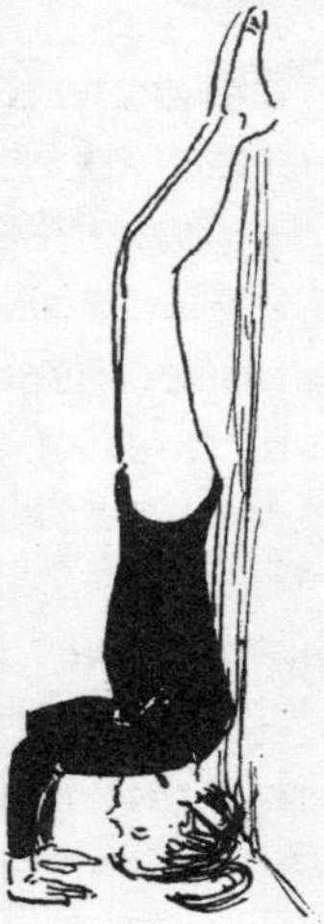

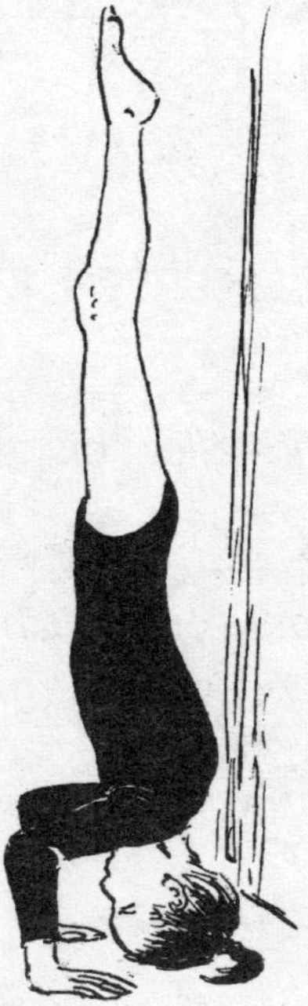

◀ **STEP 3**

When you have perfected this version of a headstand, try doing one with straight legs rather than bent ones.

Off the mat

As you get better, you can try doing both headstands and handstands without support or not against the wall of the gym. But always make sure your coach is around to help you with these more difficult stages.

Springboard

Every time you arrive at the gym you will be bubbling with enthusiasm to get going straight away. But it is important to remember that even though the gym is a place of fun, it can also be a dangerous place if you don't use it with respect. Your own coach will tell you the code of practice or rules of your own gym, but here are some basic ideas for you to think about.

- *Wear the right kit and look smart.*
- *Never wear any jewellery and keep your nails short and neat.*
- *Listen to what your coach says and follow his or her instructions.*
- *Never use a piece of apparatus until your coach says you are ready to.*
- *Never use any apparatus in the gym without supervision.*
- *Don't walk underneath or over apparatus – even if no one else is using it.*
- *Your coach will tell you how to check each piece of apparatus before use to make sure that it is safe. Make sure that you carry out your own safety checks by following their instructions.*
- *Never try to take short cuts – if you don't warm up before you start you could injure yourself.*

6 Head over heels

Cartwheels • jumps and leaps

Now you know how to balance on your head and hands and to keep control of your body while you are on the move, it's time for you to combine these skills.

What can I do next?

A natural progression from the handstand is a **cartwheel**. Think of it as going into a handstand but with your hands sideways and then continuing to move in the same direction to come out of it again.

Start in the same position as you would for a handstand, but with your leg pointed to one side. Step on to the pointed foot and bend the knee on that leg. Touch the mat with your hand and, taking your weight on that hand, push up your legs so that you swing them over your head. In the mid-way position you should have both hands on the floor and both legs in a 'V' position above you. Then you land back on your feet in the same position as you started – but with the opposite foot pointed to the side.

Off the mat

Try to do cartwheels in a straight line. Your coach may mark a line on the mat so that you can see if you are moving your cartwheel along it. As you get better, try doing two cartwheels in succession or travelling further with each wheel. You may eventually be able to do cartwheels by putting only your second hand down on the mat!

What is a round off?

A **round off** is a movement where you move forwards and turn backwards. Start by facing the direction you want to move to. Step forward and move up on to your hands, one at a time. Swing your legs through the handstand position and bring them together. Then push up from both hands and make a quarter turn, landing with both feet together and your arms up and fully flexed either side of your head.

Advanced moves

*The **back flip** is often performed as a continuation movement after a round off because you have already built up the momentum of moving backwards. But remember: like all advanced moves, the back flip should only be performed under the supervision of a qualified coach.*

Start from the standing position and move off balance backwards, then push from your feet, swinging your arms up and backwards over your head. You should arrive in an arched position just before the handstand position. The legs are snapped downwards as the arms push against the floor. Your body then snaps up to a standing position.

Advanced moves

*Another movement that moves in the same direction but without the flight is a **back walkover**. For this you start in the front scale position, move your hips forwards and your arms behind you, reaching back until you are able to take your weight on your hands. As your back arches, lift the raised leg up higher and push off from the foot that is still on the mat. At the mid-way point you should be standing on your hands with your legs in a splits shape above you. Continue to swing the first leg and then land on that foot before lifting your hands from the mat and closing the position with your feet straddled and your second leg behind you.*

Is there any difference between a jump and a leap?

Yes. A jump takes off from both feet and lands on both feet and does not aim to cover any floor area. A leap will take off from one foot, cover floor area while you are in the air and land on the other foot.

You will see gymnasts perform many different jumps and leaps in their routines, but here are some of the most common ones:

tuck jump *straddle jump* *pike jump*

star jump

stag leap

split leap

How do gymnasts jump and leap with such lightness and grace?

The first rule of good jumping is to start with good posture. The second rule is to bend your knees properly so that you can push up firmly and gain maximum height. The third rule is to land lightly, moving through your feet and with your knees bent. You can improve your own jumping by practising jumping with your arms out at your sides. Concentrate on gaining as much height as possible and on landing without making a 'thump' as you hit the mat.

7 Leap for the sky

Using a springboard • vaults • pommel horse • balance beam • rings • asymmetric bars • parallel bars • high bar

So now you've got to grips with a number of basic moves and have progressed on to rolling, jumping and leaping – well done!

I've already linked some shapes and movements together so what can I do next?

Your coach will tell you when you are ready to progress on to your first floor sequence. Depending on your ability, you may be asked to complete a compulsory set sequence as well as perhaps a voluntary sequence. But remember: you will only be able to move on to the more difficult manoeuvres if your coach gives you the go-ahead. Your coach known best!

Springboard

- *Girls perform floor sequences to music but boys don't.*
- *Boys' sequences need to be artistic even though they are not performed to music.*
- *Girls can include dance steps that interpret the mood of the music.*
- *Include jumps, leaps, balances and gymnastic movements in your routine.*
- *As you get better, include changes in direction and display your strength.*
- *Keep to the time limit you have been set – you will be penalised for going over time.*

When can I start on the other pieces of apparatus?

Only when your coach is satisfied that you have grasped the basic moves and balancing skills on the floor will he or she let you try them on the apparatus. Let's run through the basics:

The horse

Girls use the horse widthways and at a lower height (125cm) than boys. Junior gymnasts have the height adjusted, with the lowest height being 110cm. Girls usually run up to the horse from about 20m, with a maximum limit of 25m. Boys use the horse lengthways at a maximum height of 135cm and are limited to the same maximum run-up.

Work on the horse is known as vaulting and you'll use a springboard to launch you up and on to the horse.

First you will need to learn how to jump from a springboard. Take a run up to the springboard and then, with your feet together, jump up and forwards. Make sure that you bend your knees on landing with feet together, as lightly as possible on to a mat.

Off the mat

It is very important that you land on a padded mat at least 10cm thick. The mat absorbs the impact as you land and prevents injury to the knees and other joints.

The first vault to try is a **squat vault**. Run up to the board and make contact on the horse with your hands first. As you gain height, tuck your legs up underneath you as you push up from the horse. You should extend your legs and body before you land on the mat on the other side of the horse.

Off the mat

Make sure that your hands are shoulder-width apart when they land on the horse. They should be flat, with the palm completely making contact with the surface of the horse.

Now try a **straddle vault**. After leaving the springboard, reach out to the horse with your hands and bring your legs up in a straddle position. Push off from the horse with your hands and close your legs as soon as possible so that they extend before you land on both feet.

Advanced moves

*Once you have perfected the ability to gain height and speed on the horse, your coach may encourage you to try a **hand-spring vault**. With this move, by the time your hands have made contact with the horse, your entire body should be off the springboard and already propelling your body, heels over head. You'll need to land cleanly on the mat away from the apparatus.*

In competitions, girls are allowed two chances at vaulting and it is the highest of the two scores that is counted in the final scores. Boys are allowed only one attempt!

The pommel horse

The pommel horse is exclusively for the more experienced boys. Work on the pommel horse demands a great deal of strength, skill and stamina as the gymnast has to balance on one hand while he swings his legs around the handles. The pommels (or handles) can be adjusted from 41cm to 44cm apart, depending on the size of the gymnast.

When your coach thinks a gymnast is ready for work on the pommel horse, he may start with **double leg circles**. To perform these, the gymnast lifts each hand in turn as he swings his legs together around the apparatus like this:

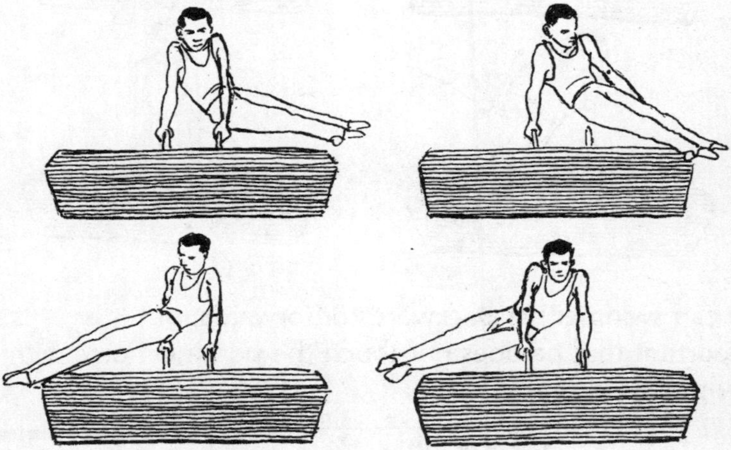

He has to keep his body as straight as possible and never let his legs or any other part of his body to touch the pommel horse.

Springboard

The pommel horse was developed by soldiers in the 19th century from the apparatus that medieval knights and soldiers sat on to learn to ride and joust!

Once the gymnast has perfected the double leg circles, he may have a go at the **shears**. This is a movement a bit like the pendulum on a clock. He has to imagine that his body is a pair of garden shears and that he is swinging the shears across the pommel horse and changing the blades (in other words his legs) at the end of every swing.

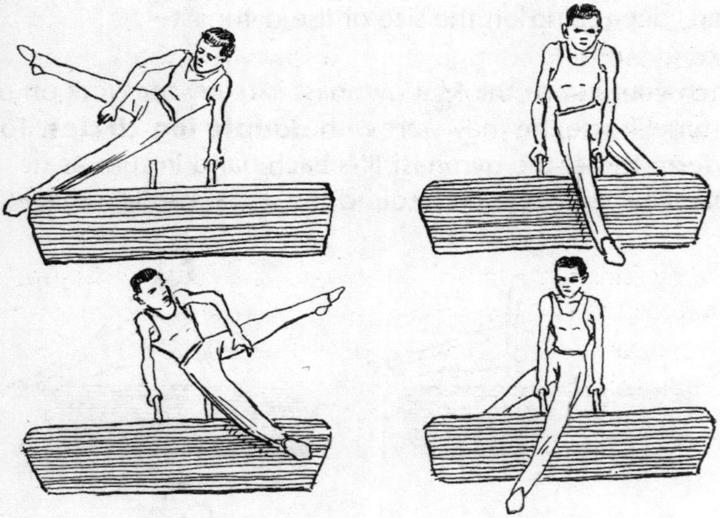

He can swing either backwards or forwards, but it is important that he does not touch the pommel horse with any part of his body.

Advanced moves

Once the gymnast is able to swing his legs around the pommel horse without touching it, he may move on to even more demanding routines. ***Flairs*** *is a circular movement using split positions of the leg. In the* ***Magyar walk****, the gymnast walks along the length of the pommel horse while continuing to keep his body away from the horse and his legs swinging around in circles.*

The balance beam

Exclusively for the girls, the balance beam is padded and covered in a non-slip surface so that gymnasts can perform the increasingly demanding manouevres that are invented by modern performers and their coaches.

First of all, you will build up confidence on the beam by walking along it, turning round and walking back again – all under the supervision of your coach! If you fall off, your fall will be cushioned by a layer of mats on the floor. Then you need to learn to mount the beam via a springboard without assistance. You can do this with a **squat mount**.

Start by facing the beam widthways and make a run-up, launching off the springboard with your feet and placing your hands on the beam. Land on the beam in a tucked position before standing upright.

Next you will learn to balance in set positions on the beam. For an **arabesque** you need to hold the position for at least two seconds.

In a **'V' sit** you will need to sit lengthwise on the beam with your hands just behind you. Extend one leg in the air with your foot pointed and keep the other bent on the beam, again with your foot pointed.

For a **'Y' balance** extend one leg out to the side and use the same arm as extended leg to hold the position. Try to keep your body as square to the front as you can while you hold the position for two seconds.

When your coach thinks you are ready, you may progress to jumping and leaping. You might even perform cartwheels, handstands, walkovers and turns!

Advanced moves

The rings

Work on the rings demands the strength and determination of the experienced male gymnast. The rings are suspended 2.5m from the floor and the gymnast is lifted up to the rings by his coach. On the rings, the gymnast performs a sequence of swings and turns from balance position to balance position.

*The **half lever** is where the gymnast pushes himself up on the rings and holds his body at an angle with the legs out in front.*

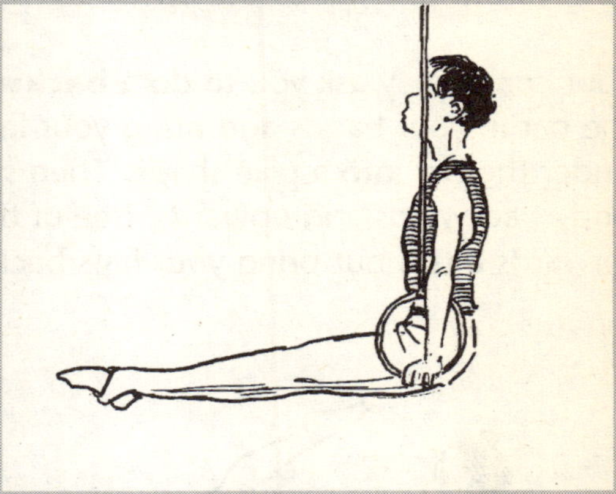

*The **crucifix** is when the gymnast balances himself with his arms out to the side and the body straight. This position is extremely difficult and requires many years of careful training.*

Asymmetric bars

The asymmetric bars are often referred to as high and low bars, or uneven parallel. This is a girls-only piece of apparatus. Your coach will only allow you to work on the asymmetric bars if you have built up great strength in your hands and shoulders. It is very tough work! Gymnasts mount the bars from either side and can do so from a springboard. The sequence includes a series of swings and jumps from one bar to the other.

Your coach may ask you to do a **backward circle**. Hold the bar in your hands and bring your legs forwards and under the bar into a pike shape. Then swing your legs and body backwards and upwards, free of the bar. Finally swing forwards again but bring your hips back into the bar.

In an **upward circle** you face the low bar and hold on to it with your palms over the top. Pull up from the floor and lift your legs forwards and upwards while at the same time bringing your hips into the bar. Finish by continuing the upward movement until your body is extended straight.

Advanced moves

With experience you will be able to create spectacular displays of swings, twists and turns and increasingly more daring under- and over-bar dismounts. Ask your coach to advise you about using handgrips to make the work easier on your hands.

The parallel bars

Another one for the boys, the routines on the parallel bars are made up of swinging movements above and below the bars with the gymnast performing handstands and stationary positions with which he can show off his sense of balance – and strength!

In the **undersomersault**, the gymnast starts above the bars and then falls into a swing under the bars before moving upwards again. He has to release his grip on the bars at one stage, only to catch them again a second later. If he is really good at this he goes on to swing up to a handstand finish.

The **straddle clip** is a tricky manouevre. Starting with either straight or bent arms, the gymnast swings his body back and pushes up on his arms to let go. He quickly opens his legs and passes them over the bars in the straddle position. As he grips the bars again behind him, he quickly brings his legs together and down between the bars.

Advanced moves

If the gymnast wants to add a twist to his routine, he can use the ***Diamidov turn****. He swings and then, from one arm, makes a full turn or twist of his body finishing in a handstand.*

Springboard

Many of the balances and manouevres in gymnastics are named after the gymnasts and coaches who invented them. The Magyar walk and the Diamidov turn are just some of the routines that we wouldn't see if they hadn't been developed to perfection by some of the world's leading gymnasts.

High bar

Some gymnasts think that this is the most spectacular of the men's apparatus. It demands swings, changes of direction and quick-release action.

With the **upstart** the gymnast needs to swing up and back raising his legs to the bar and finally bringing his body up so that he is in a straight line with the top of his body above the bar.

The **long swing** is when the gymnast swings around the bar either backwards or forwards. With each swing he needs to pass through a handstand.

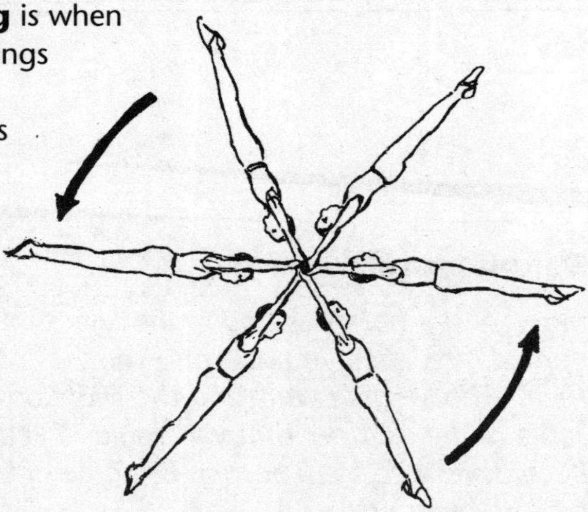

A gymnast can dismount from the bar with a **back away**. With this the gymnast swings upwards and forwards before letting go of the bar and completing a somersault. The gymnast lands on the mat, his sequence complete.

Off the mat

When a gymnast first starts work on the high bar his coach may attach him to a safety harness so that he can learn the more difficult movements without coming to any harm.

8 Rhythmic gymnastics

Rope • hoop • ribbon • ball • clubs

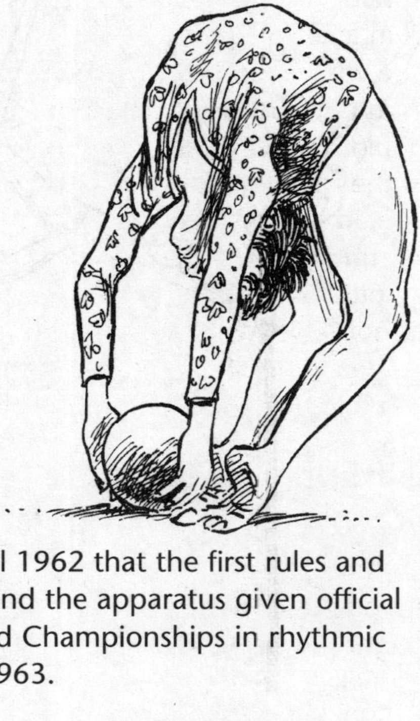

If you are a girl and you like floor work and moving to music then this could be the branch of gymnastics for you! At the beginning of the 20th century, the girls' side of gymnastics involved balancing work with clubs and dumbbells. At that time, French and German gymnasts were beginning to develop the first rhythmic gymnastic routines. But it wasn't until 1962 that the first rules and regulations were defined and the apparatus given official recognition. The first World Championships in rhythmic gymnastics were held in 1963.

What makes rhythmic gymnastics different from other girls' floor work?

Just like gymnastic floor work, rhythmics is performed to music. The big difference is that in rhythmic work you will be working with hand-held apparatus. There are five pieces of apparatus, and your coach will decide when you are ready to try working with each of the pieces.

The rope

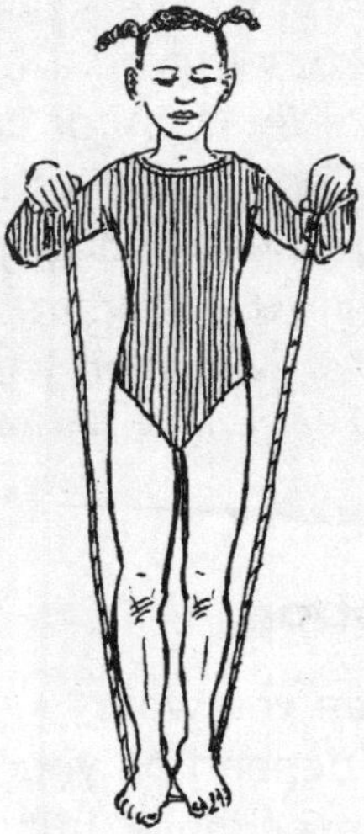

The length of the rope with which you work will depend slightly on your height, but it will probably be between 2.5m and 3m. The rope will be about 8mm thick. Ideally, you should be able to stand on the middle of the rope and hold each end under your armpits. The rope cannot have handles, but you could tie knots in the ends if that helps you work with it, or you need to make it slightly shorter.

The hoop

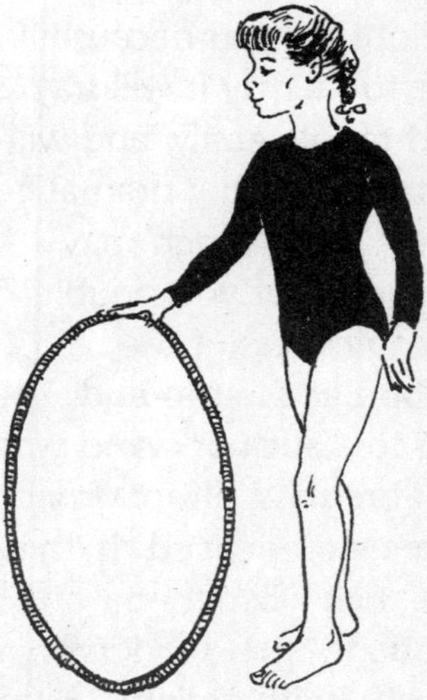

When you first start rhythmics, your coach will let you work with a lightweight plastic hoop which is usually between 80cm and 90cm in diameter. As you get more experienced in hoop work you will need to bind the hoop with coloured tape. To get the right size of hoop, stand it on the floor next to you. If it is level with your hips then it is the correct size.

Off the mat

At 13 metres square, the floor area for rhythmic work is slightly larger than for other floor work. You may practise on a conventional floor area at your gym, but don't be surprised to find the larger floor when you enter competitions! If you practise on a collection of mats at home or at your club you may find that the hoop gets stuck in the cracks between the mats!

The ribbon

The ribbon you work with will depend on your size and experience, but it can range from 3m to 7m in length and will be between 4cm and 6cm wide. It is important that the ribbon is the right weight for you because if it is too flimsy it will fray and tangle easily, and will not have such a dramatic effect. Your coach may suggest that you double the thickness of the ribbon at the top end. The ribbon is attached by a swivel pin to a stick or wand which can be made of wood, plastic or fibreglass, although fibreglass sticks are usually used by more experienced rhythmic gymnasts. Again, the length of the stick will depend on the individual gymnast but you will probably start work with a stick of about 45cm to 55cm in length, with a diameter of 7mm.

Off the mat

If you know someone who is good at DIY, perhaps they could make a ribbon and stick for you? Take a look at the ones used by the other girls at your club in order to work out how they are made. The swivel hook that you need should be available from a fishing tackle shop.

The ball

Thanks to the skills of rhythmic gymnasts, the ball looks as if it is lightweight and almost able to float on its own. In fact, it weighs a surprising 400g! You can practise with a small football or foam ball, but for display and competition work you will need to work with a proper plastic rhythmic ball, 18cm to 20cm in diameter.

Off the mat

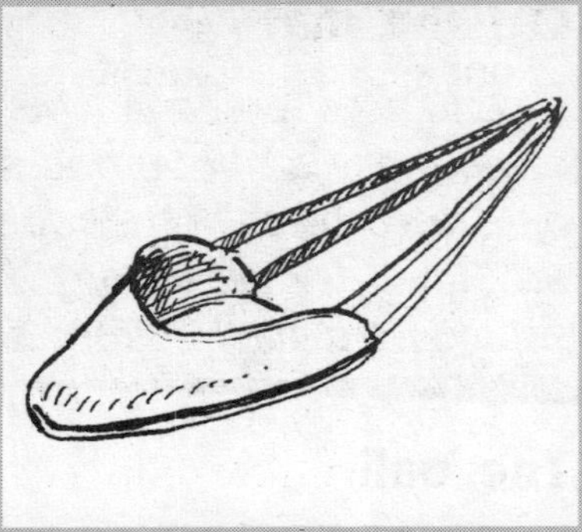

You can wear exactly the same leotard for rhythmic work as you would for all other branches of gymnastics. Many rhythmics specialists work in bare feet, but you may find it easier to work in half-shoes which are usually made of leather. Use your own experience and the advice of your coach to decide whether you need to wear them.

The clubs

The clubs are often considered to be the most difficult of the rhythmic gymnastics' apparatus, so your coach will probably leave teaching of the clubs until last. They are made from wood or plastic and their exact size will depend on your build, but they will be between 40cm and 50cm. They will each weigh a minimum of 150g.

Rhythmic gymnastics is one of the few areas of gymnastics where you will get the opportunity to work in pairs and groups (of a maximum of six). You may work in pairs within the group of six, using different pieces of apparatus which you can pass, throw and roll to each other. Group work is both challenging for the gymnast and spectacular for the audience to watch!

So what do I do with all this apparatus?

Let's start with the rope. Obviously you will perform a variety of skipping steps, but you will also need to throw the rope and then catch it as it comes back down. You can swing the rope and achieve some spectacular balances as you wrap the rope around you.

Work with the hoop will include swinging, turning, throwing and catching, jumping, and passing your body through the hoop.

Work with the ribbon includes swirls, circles, spirals, figures of eight. You can even throw and catch it.

Off the mat

It is essential to use large arm movements when you work with the ribbon to make sure that it never touches any part of your body or gets tangled up.

The ball can be rolled, balanced, bounced, thrown and caught, and circled around the body.

Work with the clubs includes swinging the clubs, circling them, throwing and catching as well as juggling them. This is the most difficult and dangerous of all the rhythmic work.

Springboard

Check out this rhythmic gymnastics skills checklist:

- *You enjoy balletic exercises and floor work.*
- *You enjoy music and interpreting your work to music.*
- *You are good at balancing.*
- *For group work you need to enjoy being part of a team and dedicated to enhancing your fellow athletes performances as well as your own.*

9 New gym sports

Sports acrobatics • sport aerobics • trampolining

There are three other gym sports that have developed over the years. One of them – sport aerobics – has emerged in only the last few years.

What exactly is sports acrobatics?

Sports acrobatics developed from the acrobatic skills of circus stars. Sports acrobatics is for boys and girls and is made up of two basic areas: tumbling and balance work. For tumbling, you'll work on a sprung tumble track 25 metres long and 1.5 metres wide. For balancing you will work on a sprung floor 12 metres square. You can work in groups: pairs, trios and in fours.

A mixed pair

A group of three girls

A group of four boys

Springboard

Sports acrobatics was officially recognised by the Olympic governing body in time for the 1986 Games.

What are the skills needed?

There are three basic exercises if you want to work in pairs and larger groups. You will need to be able to perform a set number of balances, exercises called tempo and, finally, a mixture of balance and tempo.

Off the mat

When working in groups, the gymnast at the bottom of the balance is called the base. The gymnast being supported is called the top.

In balances the base supports the top using their feet and/or hands.

A counterbalance is when one gymnast uses his or her weight to counterbalance that of another gymnast.

Off the mat

If you are the base, you should push your back into the mat to help you maintain a strong support position. Use your hands, legs and feet to take the weight of the top equally – this will make it a lot easier!

In tempo work, you perform to music. You will be thrown from your partner's shoulders and hands in a series of exciting twists and somersaults. For the combined routines, you will need to perform the most difficult and spectacular routines to catch the audience's and judge's imaginations.

In tumbling you will work on a sprung track 25m long and 1.5m wide. You will travel in a straight line performing a number of somersaults and backflips.

Off the mat

The skills you first learned as a gymnast are essential for good tumbling. Keep on practising your forward and backward somersaults, as well as your twists and turns in the air.

Acrobatic essentials

Sports acrobatics is the gym sport for you if:

- You enjoy moving quickly.
- You are good at jumping.
- You like working in pairs and groups.
- You've already got to grips with the basic gymnastic floor skills.
- You are particularly supple and strong.
- You like finding spectacularly original routines.

Off the mat

Your coach may suggest that you use a springboard to start off your tumble run. Taking off from this will give you more height and help you to build up speed.

What is sport aerobics?

There's a vast difference between an ordinary aerobics class and a sport aerobics session, although sport aerobics developed from ordinary aerobics in the early 1990s. In 1994, sport aerobics was included as an official discipline by the Féderation International Gymnastique (see page 93) and its first Olympic appearance should come in 2004.

Sport aerobics athletes have to perform to music for one minute and 45 seconds and display 16 different elements or movements, all at varying degrees of difficulty, with artistic quality. Routines need to include one-arm push-ups, one-arm-one-leg push-ups, presses, straddle jumps and one-and-a-half lateral spins in the air which land in a push-up position.

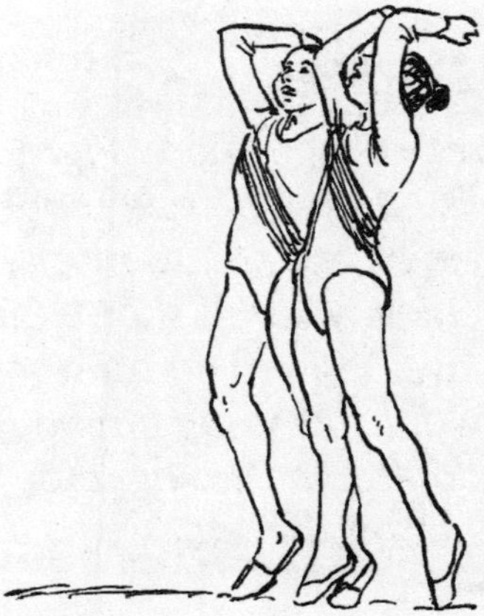

Can I do sport aerobics on my own?

You can, and you can compete either at novice, general or élite level. You can also perform as a mixed pair, trio of one sex or a small team.

Springboard

This area of gym sport is for you if:

- *You like a high octane routine.*
- *You enjoy working to music.*
- *You enjoy wearing showy outfits.*
- *You love performing on stage in shows.*
- *You want to try something relatively new.*
- *You don't mind training for hours for less than two minutes on the 'stage'.*

Sport aerobics gear

Costumes for sport aerobics are quite different from those of the other gym sports. Girls wear a one-piece costume, but it does not have sleeves and can have cut outs and a much more showy appearance. The boys wear a one-piece that has short-style legs and is sleeveless. It may also have cut-outs and be adorned with dramatic patterns and sparkling decoration. All competitors wear special aerobics shoes and short socks.

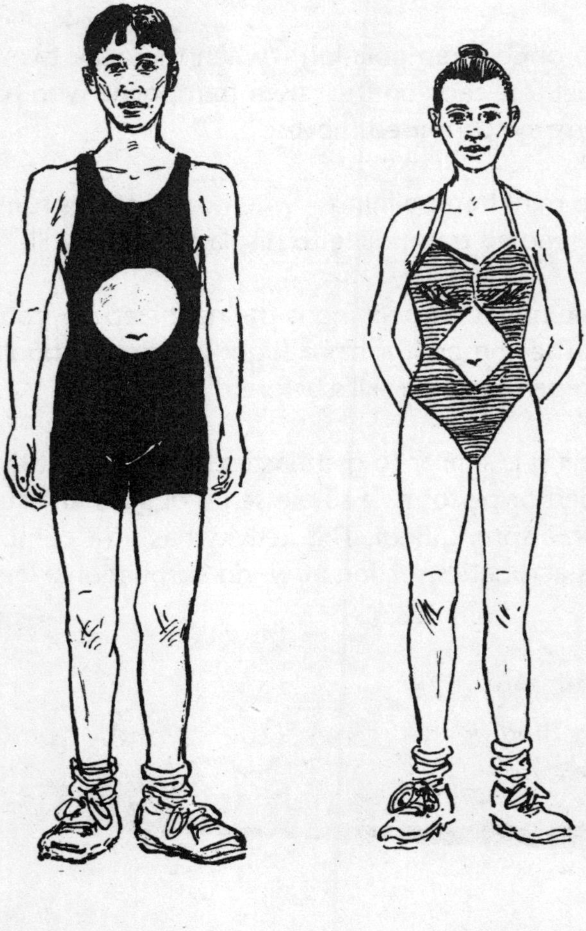

Are there any other new areas of gym sports?

Trampolining is another new area. It made its debut as an Olympic sport in the 2000 Games in Sydney as part of the gymnastics programme. There are five different disciplines in trampolining:

- Individual trampolining – when a competitor performs one compulsory routine and another which is voluntary.
- Synchronised trampolining – when there are two competitors each on their own trampoline who have to perform synchronised moves.
- Single mini trampolining – when competitors run up to a small, angled trampoline to display a single skill.
- Double mini trampolining is the next step up from single mini. The competitor has a slightly larger trampoline and has to perform two skills before dismounting.
- Tumbling is similar to gymnastics tumbling but the competitor performs a single series of skills in a straight line on a sprung floor. This activity has now combined the sports acrobatics section at world and national level.

Off the mat

Trampolining gear is identical to that of the traditional gym sports.

Trampolining tendencies

Try trampolining if:

- You've got a head for heights.
- You enjoy traditional gymnastic tumbling.
- You've mastered the basic manoeuvres and somersaults of artistic gymnastics.
- You enjoy the extra discipline of trying to work at an identical pace and height as a partner.

Springboard

Remember: you should only practise your trampolining skills under the supervision of a qualified coach.

10 Going for gold

Awards • FIG • competitions • life as a gymnast

You've practised hard and love working at the gym but where do you go from here?

Well, you already know that gym sports have made you:

- Physically fit and active
- Confident
- Happy to excel at one particular gym sport
- Anxious to know how your own particular progress is developing

Awards, badges and certificates

Your coach will encourage you to progress at the right pace for your own gymnastic ability. You will probably be encouraged to enter for badges and certificates organised either by your own club or divisional area and for the award schemes of the national gymnastics organisation of the country that you live in.

Who makes sure that everything is properly organised?

The Féderation Internationale de Gymnastique (FIG) is based in Switzerland (see page 118) and sets the rules and regulations that are followed by all major countries taking part in competitive gymnastics. FIG also acts as the major influence over international competitions such as the Olympic Games, which are held every four years.

Every country also has its own gymnastics body which will organise national competitions as well as its own award and badge schemes.

Springboard

"If another gymnast spent two hours on something, I spent 14." These are the words of Olga Korbut, Russian gymnast, who took the world by storm at the 1972 Olympics and is credited with being the person who revived international interest in gymnastics.

I'm a keen member of my local club and I've done the first of my awards, where can I go from here?

Once you have shown the skills and dedication needed to be a gymnast in any of the gym sports skills, your club coach may ask you to join your club team. If you continue to prove that you are totally dedicated and keen to move on in your sport, you may have the opportunity to climb the gym rope to success:

Once I've got into a team, what competitions may I enter?

Each area will have its own competition structure, but at first you will be encouraged to compete against teams from other schools or clubs, and it is usually from these competitions that county or state teams are created. If you are really outstanding, you may be asked to represent your county or state at a national competition. After that it is up to you to prove that you are capable of representing your country!

Springboard

"In the nine years that I trained her, she never missed even one training session, even through sickness or injury!" The words of Peggy Liddick, who coached Shannon Miller, American Olympic champion in 1996.

What are the major international competitions?

As new gym sports disciplines are added, the international competition world is frequently expanding. Here are the main competitions you will hear of and perhaps get the chance to see, either in person or on television or video.

- The **World School Games** are held every two years.
- The **World Student Games** are also held every two years.
- The **Commonwealth Games** are held every four years.
- The **Junior World Championships in Sports Acrobatics** are held every two years.
- The **Sports Acrobatics World Championships** are held every year.
- The **Rhythmic World Championships** are held every year.
- The **Artistic World Championships** are held every year.
- The **Federation of International Sport Aerobics and Fitness World Cup** is held every year.
- The **International Aerobics Federation World Cup** is held every year.
- The **Federation of International Trampolining World Cup** is held every year.
- The **Olympic Games** are held every four years.

What age must I be to compete?

Your coach will advise you about this. Artistic and rhythmic gymnastics are two of the few international sports in which younger athletes seem to excel. At the age of only 15, Nadia Comaneci, a Romanian artistic gymnast, was the first gymnast ever to score a perfect ten – something that might be matched but can never be beaten! However, even at international levels, some competitions are segregated according to age-group. Senior teams are made up of female gymnasts over the age of 15, and male gymnasts 18 and above.

The gym sports of trampolining, sports acrobatics and sport aerobics tend to attract slightly older athletes. Some athletes may have grown up through the more traditional gym sports of artistic and rhythmic gymnastics and then moved on to sport aerobics or trampolining.

I love my regular gym sessions but how can I do more – especially during the holidays?

Your coach will tell you about any training sessions that your club may run during the holidays. He or she may also be able to tell you about county, state or national training programmes which are organised to give talented gymnasts the chance to train with their country's best coaches and gymnasts. These not only give gymnasts the opportunity to work at an intensive and progressive level, they also allow gymnasts to see how their personal standard compares with other talented gymnasts.

Is training alone enough to keep me at my peak level?

There is no substitute for training hard but it is not the only thing that will help you achieve your best. Like all other athletes, you need to be sensible about your work, rest and play routine. At all times:

• Eat a sensible, healthy diet! You will need plenty of carbohydrates (pasta, bread, potatoes), at least five helpings of fresh fruit and vegetables, and a balance of vitamins and minerals. Ask your coach or your doctor to give you proper advice about a balanced diet.

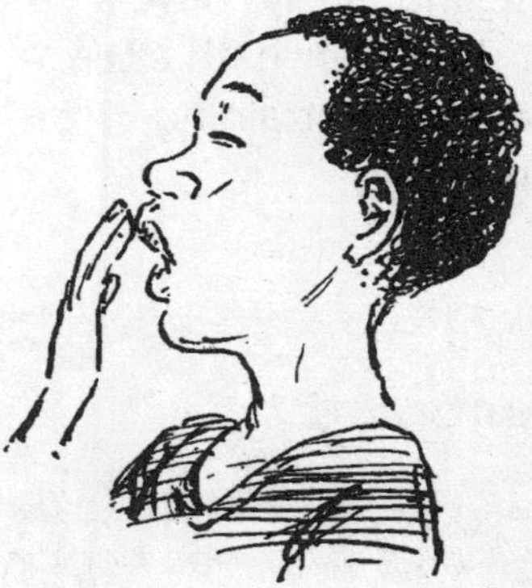

• Get some sleep! It is dangerous for you and your fellow gymnasts if you work on apparatus without being properly awake and aware. Each of us has a different sleep requirement and you will soon learn how much sleep you should aim to get every day.

• Make sure that you have time to do things other than just gymnastics. Take time out to go to the movies and see your friends – oh, and remember to do your homework, too! You will find your school is a lot more supportive of your gymnastic needs if you make sure that work at the gym doesn't make you fall behind on your school work.

• Look after your body and it will look after you! Never skip the warm-up routine that your coach has taught you before you start working on apparatus. Make sure that you wear a tracksuit as soon as you stop a training routine and always have a warm shower or bath after you have been training or competing.

Springboard

"You're not a gymnast if you're not sore," Blaine Wilson, US gymnast who was banned from his gym because he worked too hard!

What happens when I get too old for competition work and I still want to be involved in gymnastics?

Once you've been bitten by the gym bug you'll find it hard to give the sport up! As they get older, many gymnasts find that they still want to keep up the peak fitness level that their particular gym sport has given them so they continue to work out in a gym or do aerobic exercise classes. Some choose to pass on the gymnastic skills they have learned to other up-and-coming athletes by training to be a gymnastic coach or a judge. It is essential that coaches take formal training and qualifications so that they can teach at an expert level. You can find out more about training from your country's national gymnastic governing body (see pages 116-18).

Springboard

The former World Champion Olga Korbut is now in her 40s but she still practises handstands, bridges and splits every day! The former Olympic gymnast Nadia Comaneci now helps to run the Bart Conner Gymnastics Academy in Oklahoma, USA. She also performs in gymnastic displays throughout the USA in order to help raise money for charity. Vladimir Vatkin now trains the Australian men's team after giving up his own gymnastic career at only 17 because of problems with his eyesight.

Specialist work

A few special gymnasts find work in the commercial theatre world. Specialist theatrical agencies employ acrobats and gymnasts to appear in:

- pantomimes
- cabarets
- pop promo videos
- trade shows
- international musicals
- circuses

If this kind of work appeals to you, have a word with your coach, scan the Internet (see websites on pages 120-1) and read the professional theatre and gymnastics magazines for news of agencies and auditions.

11 Look out for . . .

Watching gymnastics • hall of fame

Watching world-class gymnasts competing in international competitions and exhibitions is one of the best ways to inspire yourself to improve your own gymnastic skills. Your club may organise trips to such events. If not, you may well get the chance to see these competitions on the television.

Apart from it being fun, what am I going to get out of watching competitions?

A lot – provided that you do it the right way, You can learn from watching other gymnasts if you follow the guide overleaf:

International gymnastics watching techniques

- Watch out for the way the gymnasts begin and end their routines. You can pick up new ways for mounting and dismounting as well as spectacular ways to catch the judges' eyes.
- Look out for new ways to link or group balances and movements together.
- What are the expressions on the gymnasts' faces? How are they making the audience look at them?
- Have the gymnasts introduced any new moves into their routines?
- You may get to see footage of the gymnasts warming up. Is there anything they are doing that you could copy?
- What techniques do the gymnasts use to concentrate on their routine? Can you adapt these techniques to help you?
- How do the gymnasts behave when they aren't actually performing – either waiting for their turn or perhaps receiving a medal? Remember, they are being watched by the world, so if you behave in this way at your own gym or in competitions you will be able to impress as well!
- Listen to the commentators. They have an enormous amount of knowledge about the gymnasts. They can tell you about how and where the gymnasts train, how they have improved, what their competition history is like, injuries they may have recovered from, and any new manouevres and routines they are performing.
- If the gymnasts are working to music, see how they interpret the score. Does the music just happen to be in the background, or are the gymnasts working through and with the music with their bodies and their visual expressions?

Who are the current gymnasts to look out for?

Despite the hard work and training that gymnasts put in, an injury or an unexpected fall during competition can make a gymnast either drop out of the international scene or perhaps drop down the score rankings. But look out for these gymnasts who are the stars of today and the future:

Women

Artistic

Maria Olaru, Romania
Maria has excelled at floor.

Adrienn Varga, Hungary
Adrienn has done well with both her vault and floor routines but has suffered from injuries.

Lisa Mason, Great Britain
Lisa's best work has so far been on the floor.

Trudy McIntosh, Australia
Known as the Australian pocket dynamo, look out for Trudy's spectacular vaulting.

Look out for . . .

Elena Produnova, Russia
Good all round, Elena has excelled on the floor and beam.

Olga Teslenko, Ukraine
Look out for Olga on both the bars and beam.

Simona Amanar, Romania
Excellent vaulting puts Simona high on the ranking but her floor work is also impressive.

Vanessa Atler, USA
Good work on the vault makes Vanessa one to be watched.

Zeena McLaughlin, Australia
Great all round, Zeena has recently been best on the beam and uneven bars.

Shannon Miller, USA
The former Olympic champion has a considerable record to live up to.

Svetlana Khorkina, Russia
Svetlana excels on both the floor and bars, and is an exceptional competitor.

Ludivine Furnon, France
Ludivine is a good steady all round artistic gymnast.

Rhythmic

Elena Vitrichenko, Ukraine
Elena is the one to watch with the hoop, rope and ribbons.

Julia Raskine, Bulgaria
Julia spends one-and-a-half hours practising her ballet skills before a competition!

Elena Virvichencko, Ukraine
Good all round, but especially so at the ball.

Kristy Darrah, Australia
Kristy's excellent at the ball, rope and clubs.

Yulia Barsukova, Russia
Watch Yulia perform a double pirouette spin with one leg at the side of her head, a ball held high and still with a smile on her face!

Shaneez Johnston, Australia
Shaneez is spectacular in her work with the ribbon.

Rebecca Jose, Great Britain
Rebecca's best work is seen with the hoop.

Natasha Hibbitt, Great Britain
Look out for her work with the ball and hoop.

Men

Artistic

Zoltan Supola, Hungary
Good at keeping up a high average.

Xiaopeng Li, China
Xiaopeng is amazing to watch on the floor.

Alexei Nemov, Russia
Watch out for Alexei on the floor and vault.

Marius Urzica, Romania
Marius excels at the pommel horse.

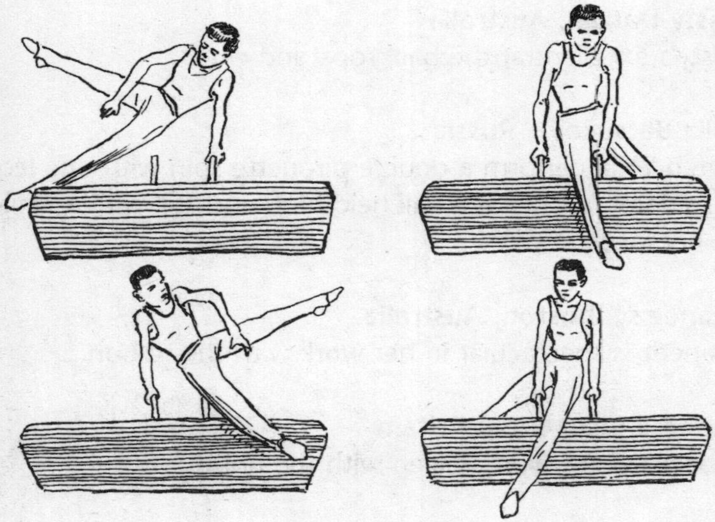

Alexei Bondarenko, Russia
Close runner to the other Russian Alexei (Nemov, see page 108) look out for this guy on the vault, floor and bars.

Pavel Mamine, Australia
Look out for Pavel on the rings.

Eric Poujade, France
Eric excels at the pommel but doesn't especially star in other apparatus.

Kanukai Jackson, Great Britain
The pommel, bars and rings are Kanukai's best.

Andrei Kravtsov, Australia
Formerly from Russia, Andrei is a great all-rounder and one to be watched.

Zhao Sheng, China
Look out for Zhao on the parallel bars.

Sports acrobatics

Mark Flores and Martyn Smith, UK
Mark and Martyn have proved their worth at men's pairs, and are world stars.

Elshan Seyfullayev,
Valery Lychkin,
Elhan Schabarzade,
Elhur Mamedov (Azerbaijan)
Top ranking in the men's four, these are four boys to keep an eye on.

Katia Antonova and Nikolai Panasuk, Russian
These two are hard to beat in the mixed pairs.

Kaat Croubels and Tine Dewaele (Belgium)
Kaat and Tine must be watched in the women's pairs.

Andrej Akinshin, Russia
A world-class tumbler.

Olena Chabenko, Ukraine
A hard-to-beat women's tumbler.

Sport aerobics

Women

Chrystelle Soulie, France
A spectacular routine has made Chrystelle a women's individual champion.

Kerry Scotts, Great Britain
A hard-worker who has already been a junior champion. Kerry could go far in the women's event.

Pat Tierney, Australia
Staggering athletic performances make this former cabaret star one of the world's best.

Men

Olivier Floris, France
Look out for him in the men's individuals.

Anthony Ikin, Australia
Tipped as a junior champ who will be a star to watch.

Mixed pairs

Dean Wright and Lisa Osborne, Australia
A spectacular duo! Just watch them in action.

Trios

Gregory Alcan, Xavier Julien and Olivior Salvan, France
A crew with dynamic moves.

Sarah Needham, Anoushka Mistry and Kelly Snape, Great Britain
Girls to watch – and be amazed!

Dale Beaumont, Justin Grahame and Jeff Lim, Australia
Tipped for a very bright future.

Off the mat

You can keep an eye on how your favourite gymnasts are doing by reading about them in the sports magazines. You can also look them up on one of the many gymnastics websites that can be found on the Internet. *Turn to pages 120-1 for more information about these.*

12 Taking a tumble or reaching for the skies?

Try this quiz to give yourself a gymnastic mind work-out to decide whether you know your back flip from your backward roll!

1 The first gymnasts performed:
a) naked b) in a leotard c) in a tracksuit

2 Which gymnast was the first to score a perfect 10?
a) Olga Korbut b) Shannon Miller c) Nadia Comaneci

3 How many gymnasts turned up at the World Gymnaestrada in 1999?
a) 3500 b) 23,000 c) 10,000

4 Gymnasts use handguards:
a) all the time b) when working on the beam
c) when working on the bars and rings

5 The floor area is:
a) 12 metres square b) 120 metres square
c) 10 metres square

6 What is this apparatus?
a) horizontal bar
b) parallel bars
c) asymmetric bars

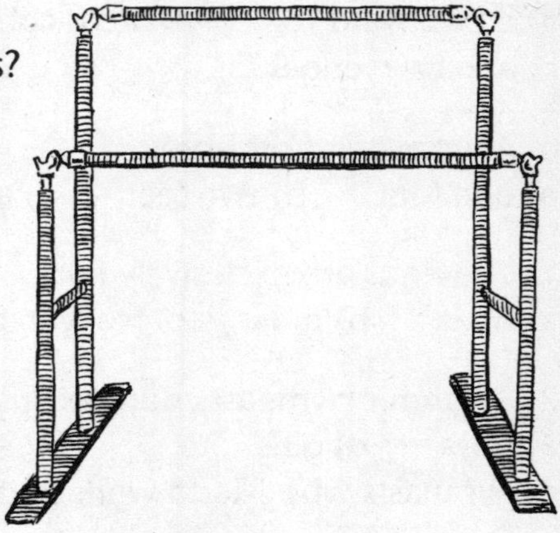

7 Before starting work on the apparatus, you should always:
a) warm up   b) take off your tracksuit
c) wait for your coach to arrive

8 What is this shape?

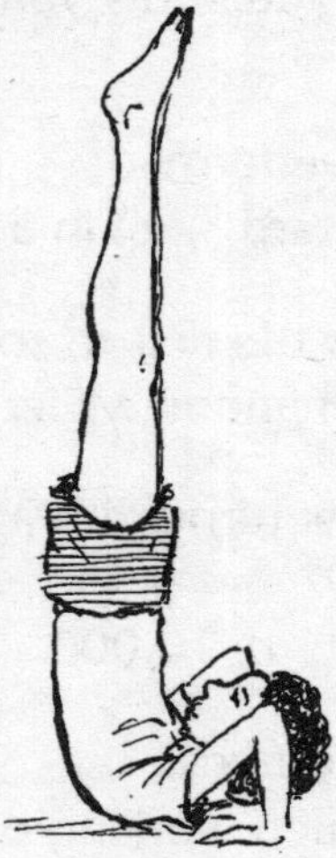

a) headstand   b) shoulder stand   c) back support

9 To help you with your rolling, your coach may let you use:
a) a backward roll   b) a chocolate roll
c) a foam wedge

10 A jump takes off from:
a) one foot   b) two feet   c) a springboard

11 The rings are exclusively for:
a) boys   b) girls   c) really experienced gymnasts

12 Rhythmic gymnastics are exclusively for:
a) boys   b) girls
c) gymnasts who like to work to music

13 Sport aerobics made its first appearance at the:
a) 1972 Olympics b) 2000 Olympics
c) 1996 Olympics

14 Where is FIG based?
a) Austria b) Bulgaria c) Switzerland

The scores

1	a) 10	b) 0	c) 0
2	a) 0	b) 0	c) 10
3	a) 0	b) 10	c) 0
4	a) 0	b) 0	c) 10
5	a) 10	b) 0	c) 0
6	a) 0	b) 0	c) 10
7	a) 0	b) 0	c) 10
8	a) 0	b) 10	c) 0
9	a) 0	b) 0	c) 10
10	a) 0	b) 10	c) 0
11	a) 10	b) 0	c) 0
12	a) 0	b) 10	c) 0
13	a) 0	b) 10	c) 0
14	a) 0	b) 0	c) 10

Total

100-140 You are a gold medallist in mind gymnastics! Well done, champ!

60-95 Keep practising! Remember to keep to the rules of your gym and watch those international competitions on video!

0-90 Perhaps go back and re-read some of the earlier chapters in the book. Those mind medals aren't beyond your reach but you've still got some training to do!

Want to know more?

The following organisations can help you to find a suitable gym and qualified coach:

British Gymnastics Association (BGA)
Ford Hall
Lilleshall National Sports Centre
Nr Newport
Shropshire TF10 9NB UK
Telephone: 01952 820330
Fax: 01952 820326
Website: http://www.baga.co.uk
BGA also runs award schemes throughout the UK. The Federation of International Trampolining recently merged with BGA.

Welsh Amateur Gymnastics Association (WAGA)
Queenswood Building
University of Cardiff
Cyncoed Campus
Cyncoed Road
Cardiff CF2 6XD Wales
Telephone: 01222 765229
Fax: 01222 765244
WAGA also run a Welsh language badge scheme.

Scottish Amateur Gymnastics Association (SGA)
Lannock Road
Woodhall Mill
Juniper Green
Edinburgh EH14 5DL
Telephone: 0131 458 5657
Fax: 0131 458 5659

Northern Ireland Amateur Gymnastics Association (NIAGA)
House of Sport
Upper Malone Road
Belfast BT9 5LA
Northern Ireland
Telephone: 01232 383813
Fax: 01232 682757 (*Make sure you make it clear that the fax is for NIAGA.*)

British Schools Gymnastics Association (BSGA)
Clive Hamilton (Secretary)
Orchard House
15 North Common Road
Uxbridge
Middlesex UB8 1PD UK
Telephone: 01895 233377
or
Joan Jackman (Chairman)
Goldrood
South Road
Brean
Somerset TA8 2SE UK
Telephone/Fax: 01278 751702
BSGA works in tandem with BGA for awards but runs competitions exclusively through schools.

Australian Gymnastics Federation
647 Burwood Road
Hawthorn East
Victoria 3123
Australia
Telephone: 613 9882 3111
Fax: 613 9882 3325
The AGF organises an extensive award scheme and training programmes.

Ontario Gymnastic Federation
1185 Eglinton Avenue East
North York
Ontario
Canada M3C 3C6
For information about Canadian gymnastics.

Féderation Internationale de Gymnastique (FIG)
Rue des Oeuches 10
Case postale 359
2740 Moutier 1
Switzerland
The FIG is the governing body for world gymnastics.

International Federation of Sports Acrobatics
Rue des Oeuches 10
Case postale 359
2740 Moutier 1
Switzerland

International Aerobics Federation and Federation of International Sport Aerobics and Fitness

For more information about these organisations and also the American National Aerobic Competitions contact:

8033 Sunset Boulevard
1420 Los Angeles
CA 90046
E-mail: nacusa@aol.com

Videos

Videos are great for inspiring you and are a good way of watching international gymnasts in stop-frame detail so that you can learn from their technique. Visit your local library to see what gymnastic videos they've got in their collection. Your coach may also be able to lend you some videos. BGA (see page 116) have a library of videos but these are mostly aimed at coaches and judges. BGA and AGF also have a merchandise catalogue which includes videos. You can find out more about these on the BGA and AGF websites (see pages 120-1). FIG has an extensive video boutique and you can contact them for their full catalogue (address on page 118). You will need to let them know which video system you need the video to work on (either PAL or SECAM) and be prepared to pay for the videos in Swiss francs.

Books

For the most up-to-date lists of books on gymnastics, contact your local library and ask them to help you find the latest publications via the microfiche or on-line. In the UK, you can also access Amazon.co.uk for on-line news about the latest books.

Websites

There are over 5000 gymnastic websites on the Internet! Check with the owner of the computer before you use their Internet user to surf the following websites.

http://www.aaog.com/
This is the American Academy of Gymnastics who have on-line news about teams, schedules and results of national and international competitions. They can also give information about where to buy clothing and equipment.

http://www.gymnastics.about.com
Everything from what to eat, the magazines to buy and what's going on in the gymnastics scene.

http://www.intlgymnast.com/
This is the on-line version of the popular *International Gymnast Magazine*.

http://www.intlgymnast.com/kidsklub/
The website where you can write, shop, and join up with other gymnasts around the world. As they say, 'If you love gymnastics you are already a member!'

http://www.ausport.gov.au/gym/home/html
News about national sports coverage and international competitions. Information about events, sponsors, magazines and merchandise.

http://www.tased.edu.au.tasonline/tas/gym/
News on Tasmanian clubs and the Tasmanian gymnastics scene and events.

http://www.ogf.com/
The latest information about Canadian gymnastics, jobs available, membership and comments from current members.

http://www.baga.co.uk
Information about BGA award schemes, coaching and judging, forthcoming events and the BGA disciplines and latest news.

http://www.Amazon.co.uk
For on-line information about the latest gymnastic books.

http://www.geocities.com.Colosseum/1264/about.html
This is the Russian gymnastics home page. At the time of going to press there wasn't much information here but it promises soon to have profiles of Russian gymnasts and information about what is happening on the Russian gymnastic scene. Keep checking it out!

http://www.milano.co.uk
For on-line information about some of the latest gymnastics gear.

http://www.geocities.com/Collosseum/Bench/6657/
All about the Irish gymnastics scene.

http://www.gymnaestrada.com
Check out the latest information on the World Gymnaestrada (see page 9 for more details).

Magazines

Magazines are a great source of inspiration and an essential way of keeping in touch with the local and international gymnastics scene.

TEN
The National Publishing Group Pty Ltd
97 Victoria Street
Potts Point
NSW 20011
Australia
Telephone: 03 9882 3111
E-mail: ausgym@ausport.gov.au

This is the official magazine of the Australian Gymnastic Federation.

The Gymnast
Unit 4
Gibbs Reed Farm
Pashley Road
Ticehurst
Wadhurst
East Sussex TN5 7HE
Telephone: 01580 200657

This is the essential magazine for the UK gymnast.

General glossary of terms

If you don't understand a gymnastic term that you've read in this book or heard on television or at the gym, look it up here!

agile Nimble, quick moving and lively. Just what a gymnast should be!
apparatus The equipment found in the gym that gymnasts use for performing.
asymmetric bars A piece of apparatus which has two bars at different heights.
Australian Gymnastics Federation (AGF) The governing body for gymnastics in Australia.
axis The gymnast's body rotates around the axis when turning or spinning.
balance The ability to keep the weight evenly distributed so that you don't wobble.
base The gymnast who remains in contact with the floor while supporting another gymnast.
bonus points You'll get these if you perform extra-difficult exercises in competitions.
British Gymnastics Association (BGA) The governing body of gymnastics in the UK.
chalk You'll use this when you want to work on the apparatus to stop your hands and feet from slipping. The chalk is made from magnesium carbonate.
choreography Your coach will choreograph a series of dance steps and movements to music for you to perform in your floor work.
compulsory exercises or routine In major competitions or when taking an award you will be asked to perform a number of set exercises.
demi pointe Rhythmic gymnasts are asked to perform on their toes or 'demi pointe'.
dismount A move to take you off an apparatus.
double back A double somersault that is in either the tucked or piked position.
extend To stretch a position right through the tips of your fingers and toes.
Féderation Internationale de Gymnastique (FIG) is the world governing body for gymnastic sports.
flexibility To be able to bend and stretch quite easily.
flic-flac A back handspring that is also known as a back flip.
flight A movement through the air either while you are working on the apparatus or while you are mounting or dismounting.
free cartwheel A cartwheel performed without using either hand.

free walkover A forward walkover performed without using either hand.
full twist A straight somersault performed with a 360° twist.
handguards Protective shields for your hands. Boys have different handguards from girls.
held balance You should hold a position for at least two seconds while you are performing.
hip circle A circle around the bar when the body is revolving around the hips.
inverted hang Hanging upside down on rings with legs straight upwards between the straps.
line The shape made by your body while you are performing.
lunge When you position one foot in front of the other and, with the front knee bent, you lean forwards, placing most of your weight on the front foot.
mount The move to get you on to an apparatus.
pike The position when your body is bent at the hips into a V-shape.
pirouette A spin made about your hands or feet.
planche Horizontal support of your body on your hands when working on the rings, beam, parallel beam or floor.
posture The way you hold your body.
rebound When you bounce from a springboard on to another piece of apparatus.
release and catch When you let go of an apparatus, turn or move in mid-air, and then catch the apparatus again.
round off A way to reverse direction from forwards to backwards when you are on the move.
routine A complete series of exercises and movements performed by a gymnast.
scissors On the pommel horse, when both legs are spread and cross the horse while performing single circles.
sequence A series of movements linked together.
somersault A movement in which the body turns 360° in the air.
straddle When both legs are wide apart to clear apparatus.
suppleness The ability to use the entire body without hindrance and with loose joints and flexible muscles.
top The gymnast who is supported during a routine by the base gymnast.
tuck To bring your knees up to your chest.
voluntary exercises A routine in which the exercises and movements are chosen by the gymnast and the coach rather than decided by a governing body.
warm up The essential routine at the start of every training session.

Index

acrobatic gymnasts 110
Akinshin, Andrej 110
Alcan, Gregory 112
Amanar, Simona 106
Antonova, Katia 110
apparatus 19-25, 60-73
arch 33
artistic gymnastics 19-73
artistic gymnasts 105-106, 108-109
Artistic World Championships 96
asymmetric bars 21, 68-9
Atler, Vanessa 106
Australian Gymnastics Federation 12, 117
awards 92

back away 73
back flip 55
back scale 32
back support 35
back walkover 56
backward circle 68
backward roll 44
badges 92
balance beam 24, 65-6
balancing 39, 85
ball 77, 81
ballet 40
Barsukova, Yulia 107
base 85
basic shapes 32-8
Beaumont, Dale 112
Bondarenko, Alexei 109
books 119
bridge 36
British Gymnastics Association (BGA) 116
British Schools Gymnastics Association 117

cartwheel 53, 54
certificates 92
Chabenko, Olena 110
circle roll 48
clothing 14-15, 89
clubs 17, 18, 78, 81
coach 15-18, 101
Comaneci, Nadia 11, 97, 101
Commonwealth Games 96
Croubels, Kaat 110

Darrah, Kristy 107
Dewaele, Tine 110
Diamidov 71
diet 99
dish 33
double leg circles 63

Federation of International Sport Aerobics and Fitness 118
Federation of International Sport Aerobics and Fitness World Cup 96
Federation of International Trampolining World Cup 96
Féderation Internationale de Gymnastique (FIG) 93, 118
flairs 64
floor 20, 76
Flores, Mark 110
Floris, Olivier 111
foam wedge 45
forward roll 45-6
front scale 32, 56
front support 35
Furnon, Ludivine 106

Grahame, Justin 112
Greeks 6, 7
group work 79, 88

hair 16
half lever 67
half roll 43
half shoe 78
handspring vault 62
handstand 49, 51
headstand 50-1
Hibbitt, Natasha 107
high bar 72-3
hoop 75, 80
horizontal bar 22
horse 22, 59

Ikin, Anthony 111
International Aerobics Federation 118
International Aerobics Federation World Cup 96
International Federation of Sports Acrobatics 118

Jackson, Kanukai 109
Jahn, Friedrich Ludwich 8, 9
jewellery 16
Johnston, Shaneez 107

Jose, Rebecca 107
Julien, Xavier 112
Junior World Championships 96

Khorkina, Svetlana 106
Korbut, Olga 10, 11, 93, 101
Kravtsov, Andrei 109

'L' lie 34
'L' sit piked 34
'L' sit straddled 34, 48
Leotard, Jules 15
Li, Xiaopeng 108
Liddick, Peggy 95
Lim, Jeff 112
Ling, Pehr Henrik 8, 9
log roll 47
long swing 72
Lychkin, Valery 110

McIntosh, Trudy 105
McLaughlin, Zeena 106
magazines 122
Magyar walk 64, 71
Mamedov, Elhur 110
Mamine, Pavel 109
Mason, Lisa 105
Miller, Shannon 11, 95, 106
Mistry, Anoushka 112

Needham, Sarah 112
Nemov, Alexei 108
Northern Ireland Amateur Gymnastics Association 117

Olaru, Maria 105
Olympic Games 6, 7, 9, 10, 87, 93, 96
Ontario Gymnastic Federation 118
Osborne, Lisa 111

pairs 79, 83, 88
Panasuk, Nikolai 110
parallel bars 22, 69-70
pommel horse 24, 63
Poujade, Eric 109
Produnova, Elena 106

quiz 113-14

Raskine, Julia 107
rhythmic gymnastics 19, 74-82
rhythmic gymnasts 107
Rhythmic World Championships 96
ribbon 76, 80
rings 25, 67
Romans 6, 7
rope 75, 79
round off 54
Russian lever 38

Salvan, Olivior 112
Schabarzade, Elham 110
Scottish Amateur Gymnastics Association 116
Scotts, Kerry 111
Seyfullayev, Elshan 110
shears 64
Sheng, Zhao 109
shoes 15, 78
shoulder stand 36
sleep 99
Smith, Martyn 110
Snape, Kelly 112
Soulie, Chrystelle 111
springboard 25
sport acrobatics 19, 83-91
Sport Acrobatics World Championships 96
sport aerobics 87-9
sport aerobics gymnasts 111-12
spotting 50
squat mount 65
squat vault 61
straddle clip 70
straddle hold 38
straddle position 70
straddle vault 62
Supola, Zoltan 108
Swedish drill 8

tempo 85, 86
Teslenko, Olga 106
Tierney, Pat 111
top 85
trampolining 90-1
trios 84, 88
tumbling 83, 86

undersomersault 70
upstart 72
upward circle 69
Urzica, Marius 108

'V' sit 66
'V' sit balance 41
Varga, Adrienn 105
Vatkin, Vladimir 101
videos 119
Vitrichenko, Elena 107

warm-up exercises 26-31
websites 120-1
Welsh Amateur Gymnastics Association 116
World Gymnaestrada 9, 121
World School Games 96
World Student Games 96
Wright, Dean 111

'Y' balance 66

super.activ

0 340 773294	Acting	£3.99	☐
0 340 764686	Athletics	£3.99	☐
0 340 736305	Basketball	£3.99	☐
0 340 715189	Cartooning	£3.99	☐
0 340 736496	Chess	£3.99	☐
0 340 715200	Computers Unlimited	£3.99	☐
0 340 736275	Cricket	£3.99	☐
0 340 715219	Drawing	£3.99	☐
0 340 736313	Film-making	£3.99	☐
0 340 736291	Fishing	£3.99	☐
0 340 715138	Football	£3.99	☐
0 340 76466X	Golf	£3.99	☐
0 340 778970	Gymnastics	£3.99	☐
0 340 736321	In-line Skating	£3.99	☐
0 340 749504	Karate	£3.99	☐
0 340 715146	The Internet	£3.99	☐
0 340 736267	Memory Workout	£3.99	☐
0 340 736283	Pop Music	£3.99	☐
0 340 715170	Riding	£3.99	☐
0 340 791659	Rugby	£3.99	☐
0 340 715235	Skateboarding	£3.99	☐
0 340 736526	Snowboarding	£3.99	☐
0 340 71512X	Swimming	£3.99	☐
0 340 764465	Tennis	£3.99	☐
0 340 773332	Writing	£3.99	☐
0 340 73650X	Your Own Website	£3.99	☐

Turn the page to find out how to order these books.

ORDER FORM

Books in the **super.activ** series are available at your local bookshops, or can be ordered direct from the publisher. A complete list of titles is given on the previous page. Just tick the titles you want and complete the details below. Prices and availability are subject to change without prior notice.

Please enclose a cheque or postal order made payable to Bookpoint Ltd, and send to: Hodder Children's Books, Cash Sales Dept, Bookpoint, 39 Milton Park, Abingdon, Oxon OX14 4TD. Email address: orders@bookpoint.co.uk.

If you would prefer to pay by credit card, our call centre team would be delighted to take your order by telephone. Our direct line is 01235 400414 (lines open 9.00 am – 6.00 pm, Monday to Saturday; 24-hour message answering service). Alternatively you can send a fax on 01235 400454.

Title .... First name .... Surname ....

Address ....

....

....

Daytime tel .... Postcode ....

If you would prefer to post a credit card order, please complete the following.

Please debit my Visa/Access/Diner's Card/American Express (delete as applicable) card number:

Signature ....

Expiry Date ....

If you would NOT like to receive further information on our products, please tick ☐.